A LARGER SILENCE

A
LARGER SILENCE

Yvonne Burgess

PENGUIN BOOKS

20087659

PENGUIN BOOKS

Published by the Penguin Group
27 Wrights Lane, London W8 5TZ, England
Penguin Putnam Inc, 375 Hudson Street, New York, New York 10014,
USA
Penguin Books Australia Ltd, Ringwood, Victoria, Australia
Penguin Books (NZ) Ltd, Cnr Rosedale and Airborne Roads, Albany,
Auckland, New Zealand
Penguin Books India (P) Ltd, 11 Community Centre, Panchsheel Park,
New Delhi – 110 017, India
Penguin Books (South Africa) (Pty) Ltd, 5 Watkins Street, Denver Ext 4,
Johannesburg 2094, South Africa

Penguin Books (South Africa) (Pty) Ltd, Registered Offices:
Second Floor, 90 Rivonia Road, Sandton 2196, South Africa

First published by Penguin Books (South Africa) (Pty) Ltd 2000

ISBN 0 140 29564 X

Typeset by PJT Design in 11.5/13.5 point Bodoni
Cover design: Bureau Connexion
Printed and bound by Interpak Natal

For Frederick Oughton
old friend and, like Gladstone,
A Teller of Tales

ONE

PULLED IN

When they finally pulled him in he needed hospitalisation so they put him in a big white bed in which his emaciated frame, little more than skin and bone, hardly tented the sheets. He half sat up against the pillows most of the time, eyes round and wide and staring straight ahead. He must have been in a state of shock or bewilderment or surprise, who knew?

Because for the first few days he said nothing. His jaw hung slackly and his mouth, with craggy teeth and horizontal overlap, looked like the entrance of a small, dark cave.

And that was the way of it until the nourishment dispensed drop by drop straight into his stringy veins began to take effect and he began to fill out, turning from parchment to pink, his eyes beginning to reflect light and to move, to see, to respond almost intelligently.

They had combed his hair (too long now, wispy and white) with a wet comb, so that the thin strands stuck together and strips of pink skull showed through. They had shaved him as well, but left, at his pitiable pleading, the promise of a moustache. Spiky and white, not quite symmetrical – a little unbalanced, in fact, being noticeably thinner and longer on one side – but a moustache none the less; and besides it was difficult to judge, unless one stood squarely at the bottom of the bed.

So he lay, day after day, tended by large nurses in tight white uniforms which rode up over their extended rumps, and small chirpy nuns, most of them as old and frail as their charges, their order having failed to attract many postulants in recent years and they, therefore, a dying breed themselves.

For some time after he'd been pulled in he had rambled in a feverish, disjointed way about what he called, with a crooked, pained smile, the 'brotherhood of the road'; of how he'd been prepared to do anything to survive, old soldier that he was and inured to hardship, but that he'd drawn the line at eating Koksie Harmse's stewed cat and drinking meths diluted with Mix Eleven and water. Rather starve, he'd said.

And so, of course, he very nearly had.

He also rambled on about a number of women: Evadne, Mavis, Anna – sometimes Annie – and a girl, Lillith; but enquiries among the vagrants in the public parks instituted by the welfare services yielded no clues as to their identities – wife, sisters, a daughter? – nor could he enlighten them, disoriented as he still was.

The matter was handed to the police eventually and the Salvation Army and they, fortunately, came up with a few facts: he was Rudyard Kipling Knoesen, one-time inmate of a State Work Colony, one-time awaiting-trial prisoner, later certified a depressive sociopath and twice detained in a State Mental Hospital at the President's pleasure.

With the link to the State's Mental Health Services thus established, and through the good offices of the Chief Psychiatrist – who may or may not have been pricked in his conscience regarding what may have been a premature discharge from a psychiatric Aftercare Centre – Rudyard Kipling Knoesen was declared an ailing indigent with neither family nor viable means of support, and placed in a Home for the Aged run by the Roman Catholic Church, he having previously designated himself a Roman Catholic, albeit lapsed – an extremely fortuitous circumstance, since, if he had not been accepted he would undoubtedly have been reduced to eating some of Koksie's concoctions sooner or later.

So here he was in the Home and, from what he had seen so far, in the company of old women who shuffled about in slippers, and a few, a very few, old men like himself, and eating what he later said may not have been cat, but looked and tasted as if it were.

But of course he was grateful for having been pulled in. The memory of his many deprivations while on the road (although strictly speaking he had never really been on the road; he had only been in the park) had haunted him until latterly when his memory, mercifully, began to develop large blank patches, becoming like a pool in which images, some recognisable, some not, floated in and out without much reference to conscious thought processes.

He didn't want to remember where he'd been, the cheap hotels, sleeping on broken bedsprings, in Salvation Army hostels and even, one unforgettably humiliating night, in the doorway of a pharmacy.

Best forgotten of course; and so, expedient to the end, and pragmatic as always, he allowed his memory, like his religion, to lapse, recalling unrelated events and people quite arbitrarily; like his friend Annie, the dear girl who had suffered from bipolar affective disorder. Annie of fond memory, or what was left of it.

But every now and then he would be able to remember things with disconcerting clarity; the connection would be made as neurons vaulted synapses and he would all but taste it again:

the sickly sweet Jerepigo, Muscadel, or Hanepoot, with whatever they had added to give it 'skop' as Zolah used to say. It
could kill, the stuff they drank; it could blind one, cause
aneurysms all over the brain, veins popping like balloons as
the fumes filled and ruptured them. Not the way he'd ever
wanted to go, sodden and senseless.

Suddenly he heard Annie again: *This isn't the way.*

Damn right, he thought, screwing his eyes up against the
pain behind his eyeballs and seeing her as he had seen her
last, ethereal in white. She'd never worn white before. Dazzling
against her pale skin; white on white, with that flaming mane
of hers. Why hadn't she realised how striking she was? And
what had she said about resembling the Flanders Mare? Or
Anne of Cleves? Anne of my heart, he should have told her.
But maybe he had?

Always putting herself down. Annie, too young and too good
for him. Too poor; although she may have stood to inherit . . .
Too late now, anyway. He struggled to put her out of his mind
because thinking about her made the pain worse. Right up into
his sinuses now, as if he'd been sniffing fire.

What had crazy Zolah put into the sherry? It had been more
than the usual meths. Ethyl alcohol? Surgical spirits? After-
shave? The woman was a misanthropist, like all whores. She
had a death wish, trying to kill them all . . .

Because instead of going with Annie he'd chosen, in his
madness, Claude. Claude, like a large crow in his dirty flapping
rags, bedraggled and bedevilled. Claude and his cronies: Koksie
Harmse and Fatarse or Fartarse (both had been applicable)
Froelich, also known as 'ou Floors'. And Zolah, who'd simply
begun to tag along with them, for protection, perhaps; or for
the acceptance she could not find anywhere else.

But he'd never really been one of them, he knew that; not
the way they eyed him thoughtfully, obviously wondering

whether the association could be turned to their advantage in some way; financial preferably. Cash or kind. His jacket hadn't been too bad. Nor his shoes.

He'd have been no match for them and so, when he felt matters coming to a head, he had pointed to his flies and some bushes on the far side of the greenhouse and veered off, away from them, squinting first with one eye then the other, trying to focus, taking a crablike route because for some reason his right leg had locked at the hip, and was behaving like an oar, forcing him to proceed in circles. He'd had to battle to get away from them, every inch of the way, trying to devise a plan but finding that his brain was in no better shape than his eyes or his leg.

Even now, just remembering started the clamour in his head, a pounding, agonising conflict as though the right and left sides of his brain had become detached and were rubbing up against each other like tectonic plates, causing seismic shocks and tremors.

A bloody continental drift going on in my head, he thought, expecting his skull to explode at any moment, to erupt, blowing his brains to kingdom come.

He leaned back against the pillows to calm himself and to try to think: first things first. His suitcase. He hadn't sold it, had he? Not that the contents were all that valuable; but the suitcase itself was worth something. It was an antique. A leather relic from bygone days. Nicked from Evadne, when he decamped, before the breakdown. The first breakdown. And maybe it would help, he told himself, to get things in chronological order; maybe it would ease the friction between the plates . . .

All right then. He'd had no choice to speak of. It was Claude and the gang, or find himself another Mavis, she of the sweaty, really rank armpits and quivering bosom, the straining silk blouse, cheap brooch and even cheaper perfume.

Or even go back to old Mave herself? Could he bring himself

to go into that house again, that large pink pile she'd turned into a boarding-house after the death of her husband, the Captain, with its big pink maw of an entrance hall which swallowed one before Mave began the digesting, the rendering down?

If she would have him back; which she swore she wouldn't. 'Over my dead body,' she'd said. He might have risked it but if it really were over her dead body her kids would have thrown him out in any case.

He remembered her smell again, the sweat with the heavy overlay of floral perfume. Carnation it had been. 'My crook scent', she'd called it. Maybe she'd fancied herself a bit of a moll, because by all accounts the late Captain had been into several shady deals, one of them resulting in the acquisition of the big pink pile, the shelter, the refuge which she had used as bait to snare him, knowing he had had no other recourse.

Because it had all been too much for him, trying to get his rent together, and something in advance, perhaps, to charm her into letting him back in the interim, as a boarder, nothing more, so help him, only as a boarder . . .

Rudy gave an involuntary yelp as a sharp stab of pain in his back nearly tipped him off the bed. Kidneys, probably. Or the thought of ever having to go back to Mavis, or someone like her.

There had probably been more efficient ways to conduct the peripatetic existence he had latterly been obliged to lead, but then, when it came to really being on his uppers, Rudy had always been a novice, a dilettante, simply improvising as he went along, making a virtue of necessity, hoping earnestly that it would all come to an end and that he would once again enter some sort of comfort zone where someone, anyone, would care for him.

And mercifully it was just then that he had been pulled in to a bed in the Home, run, as he had gathered, by the Sisters Mary.

He asked them about his suitcase, his precious suitcase, the one containing his four black notebooks, his mother's slim, badly foxed volume of verse, the photograph by Debenham, the Professor of Tonsorial Artistics' onyx studs and cuff-links and framed accolade (which he'd managed to trace to a neighbourhood junk shop), together with his own meagre effects.

Like a refugee, he thought. My whole long life, everything I am and have, in one nicked leather suitcase.

And yes, they had it, they said. He'd been lying on it when they pulled him in. He smiled. Lying on it. Protecting it with his own life. Perhaps the pain in his back was due to no more than that, a bruise from lying on the suitcase? Maybe he was all right after all. Maybe his kidneys, and even his liver, hadn't quite packed in yet?

When he was finally up and about again, one of the nurses came to take him to his room and he wondered that the place looked so familiar, the long passages intersecting at small lounges; the dining-room, the Matron's and staff offices and restrooms, the dispensary and sickbays, all polished tiles and brass handrails, with doors along either side of the passages.

But then, all institutions were much the same, especially charitable and State institutions; and at least he had his own room, with his own neat little nameplate.

One of the Sisters Mary had come along to see if she'd got the spelling right. She'd written Mr R K Knoesen but after Rudy had protested, pouted and sulked for a few hours she'd relented. What did it matter, after all, as long as it made the old man happy? And so there it was: COLONEL R K KNOESEN (retd).

He had his own little cubicle (calling it a room was a trifle hyperbolic), and his own nameplate. He belonged.

At the end of his passage he discovered a small lounge where no one ever sat. It seemed to be used exclusively for funeral teas of which there were many. Not surprising, of course, since everyone there was so old, all living on borrowed time, as they informed him, if threescore and ten were indeed the allotted lifespan, or fourscore, by reason of strength.

Only what strength, Rudy wondered. There was nothing to them but nodding heads and endlessly masticating gums, like a flock of ancient sheep . . .

At the end of the other wing, and just past the dining-room, was another, bigger sitting-room where most of them did congregate day after day, while those who had arrived too late had to be content with the closed-in veranda where, inexplicably, all the chairs had been placed against the partitions under the windows so that they had to sit facing inward with nothing to look at but rows of linen cupboards.

No one seemed to care. Too old probably. Especially the women. Old beyond being women, dressed in crimplene and shiny celanese and orlon twinsets. He felt caught in some strange time-warp. It was the forties and fifties all over again. And the sixties, if one took the nurses into account. Tunics above the knees, all of them, even the blacks, although he had heard that it was considered shameful for Xhosa women to expose the backs of their knees.

Not the sort of thing one should be asking about, he didn't think, especially in the new dispensation.

They were a pleasant lot anyway, amply endowed with flesh and voice, passing unintelligible jokes down the length of the passages, together with observations about him, Rudy, and the others; things they found hugely amusing. Not that he minded; it would be laugh or cry, nothing else for it in that place, as he soon saw.

Because that was it: the lounge and passages bristling with walking sticks, wheelchairs and walkers, with old women bent double, hugging their concave or bulbous bosoms; and old nuns in the new skirts just above their burst- and varicose-veined calves, with sandalled feet revealing bunions and corns and other deformities he couldn't even name.

He'd only seen one or two white nurses and they were all on the far side of forty.

Didn't young girls become nurses any more, he wondered? Or didn't the young ones want to work in old-age homes?

Wouldn't his last days have been immeasurably brightened by a bevy of giggling young nurses – student nurses, preferably – with tight little titties and tails, or boobies and buns as they called them these days. Rudy sighed. Fate had always cata-pulted him into the arms of older women. Older women who had wanted to mother him and since older women tended to be better endowed, at least financially, he had as always taken the line of least resistance.

Little student nurses would be part of his final fantasies, as little ballerinas in tutus just skimming their little round rumps had once been.

Because in that place even the cat was old and sway-backed, lumbering along with its legs out of alignment. Needed a walker or a wheelchair like the old harpies, he thought; although not unkindly, because who was he to criticise, stringy old man that he had become, as weathered as the rest of them, as weak and quavery with his whispery voice and fluttery, prominently veined hands; still on the hoof perhaps, but only just, shuffling along like an old Chinawoman on bound feet.

There were others far worse, though; men and women who looked like the forgotten inmates of a war veterans' hospital, maimed and mutilated, some with one leg, some with half, some with none at all, squatting grotesquely on the base of their truncated bodies. The result of fractures, apparently, of diabetes, embolisms, gangrene . . . Sexless, their features barely distinguishable under their knitted caps, like aged Noddys,

9

with opaque eyes and drooling mouths, obsessed with the obscure details of their lives, endlessly repeating their tales, reminding him of the ancient mariner (even the women; in fact, especially the women) weather-beaten, desiccated, salt encrusted (or at least suffering from dreadfully dry skins), peeling like old lumber, warts and wens like barnacles on their bony cheeks and chins.

He listened to their compulsive story-telling without hearing much, his attention span erratic, the stories barely heard, with much that was vital missing (or were they leaving out many of the vital parts?). But he preferred it that way; it made what he did hear that much more curious and evocative.

They'd all lived too long, but were any of them ready to die? What made a man ready to die, Rudy wondered. That was the question. He'd have to consider it, sooner or later, and preferably before he himself felt the Grim Reaper's fetid breath . . .

In the mean time, there were the other fetid smells to consider: sourish smells, disinfectants, medications, food, with an overlay of body odours, urine, even excreta sometimes, rising from their clothes, carried on their breath . . .

Of course he, Rudy, wasn't incontinent yet, unlike many of them whose functions, uncontrolled and unselfconscious, caused acrid, nose-twitching smells to emanate from the beds, the chairs, the saturated mattresses and damp upholstery – damage done before the waterproofs could be brought out.

Why had he become so conscious of it? Was the olfactory organ in the business of compensating when the other senses began to fail?

Some of them gave the appearance of being human, walking, talking, eating, sleeping, but even they were well on the way to becoming a sub-species, something less than men and women, on their way out . . . all but blind, and deaf as both jambs of a doorcase . . .

But how much of that was genuine? Hadn't they all begun hearing only what they wanted to hear? Wasn't he learning to do that as well?

He had always had one reasonably good ear. The other drum had calcified long ago, the result of ear infections which his mother had treated with warmed sweet oil.

He remembered the occasions well – the sharp stabs of pain, his yells and then the oil poured carefully into a teaspoon blackened underneath from many similar operations, the match lit and the oil warmed before he'd have to lie down on his mother's lap, ailing ear up – the right one usually – for it to be poured in.

Ah well, no blame attached, no recriminations, no hard feelings, even. It was before the advent of antibiotics, after all, when every mother did as she saw fit and as best she could.

He'd surprised himself with the sudden memory of his mother. Perhaps that would be the way of it then; with nothing too interesting coming in from the outside, he'd be left with the interior life for stimulation, his own reflections and cogitations which he'd always found engrossing enough and perhaps, in that place, in the complete absence of other distractions, he would really be able to think and even express his thoughts again?

He'd ask for paper and a ballpoint and get down to it; some time soon, he promised himself, because, whichever way one looked at it, if he was ever going to produce anything it was now or never, that being in the very nature of things if allotted lifespans were to be taken into account.

TWO

SETTLING DOWN

There was something awful, almost obscene, about the aged, Rudy had decided. Gibbering, slavering, gnashing their gums, or grinding what was left of their teeth, eyes swivelling dumbly; they were like cattle when they caught a whiff of blood at the abattoir and wanted to stampede, but couldn't . . .

Still, he wasn't complaining. He had his own little room with a small shared bathroom on the side. Or water-closet, properly speaking, since it contained only a toilet and hand-basin, their twice weekly baths being taken in the big communal bathrooms which were fitted with all sorts of chrome handles and pulleys so that the really frail or crippled could be safely lowered into the water or on to toilet seats.

He might have been very happy there; he was being taken care of, he had a home, bed and food. He was grateful. But on the downside he hadn't yet found anyone to talk to, share observations with, about the place, its inmates, and the daily happenings; no one as congenial as Annie for instance.

That was the worst of it, with the quality of the food coming a close second.

Invalid cooking for the most part, bland baked custards and insipid steamed fish smothered in a greyish-white sauce which looked like dog's vomitus, especially on days when they'd added what might have been parsley but looked for all the world like the blades of grass dogs and cats used as an emetic . . .

Still, looking on the bright side, the Home was set in the old heart of the city not too far from the Centre where – looking back on it now, at any rate – he'd spent the happiest time of his life, philosophising with Annie, argy-bargying back and forth . . .

But there was no point in complaining. One had to be content. There was nothing else for it, seeing that one couldn't get out, except in a wooden box, as one of the staff had told him with brutal frankness when he'd enquired. Well, not with intentional brutality, perhaps, but very frankly anyway:

'Hokaay, in a box, you hear? A coffing,' she had said. Laetitia her name was, and responsible for cleaning his room, together with the others on his side of the corridor.

So there he was, and there he would obviously stay – no one else would have him now, he knew that – and he'd end up like the others, as mindless, chomping on his gums, wetting his bed, faeces on his fingers – which happened sometimes, he'd heard, when they became constipated and tried to assist nature by unplugging themselves.

He'd have to discipline himself, he saw that. He'd have to keep a tight grip on his mind, keep exercising it, by devising plots for screenplays, or something. Impossible to actually write just yet of course; he was barely able to think beyond a title or two. 'Puns and Rubbers' for instance, for a sex-farce.

He chuckled for a while, until he found he couldn't think of any other titles with which to continue the game, not even the most famous, the ones everyone knew, no matter how hard he tried; and that, he supposed, was a measure of the deterioration that had already set in, turning his grey matter to mush.

He strolled up to a little knot of wheelchairs, looked from face to face, encountering a uniform blankness, with just a hint of suspicion.

'I say,' he said, 'that novel, the one by Lawrence, you know, the one about the gamekeeper and . . .'

Suspicion deepened, turned to apprehension, the twisted, gnarled fingers beginning to grope for the wheels, ready to make a quick getaway if necessary.

He smiled at the thought of it, saw the wheelchairs suddenly scattering, getting into gear, whizzing away. The chase, as only Mack Sennett could have filmed it. He began to laugh out loud.

'Lawrence, you know, and all that . . .' he spluttered.

And then they did scatter, bumping into each other, trying to back off and be off, staring at him in wild alarm.

Why? Didn't anyone ever laugh in that place? Had they forgotten about laughter, how to be gay?

He'd had to jump out of the way or be run down.

'Just what are you up to, Colonel Knoesen?'

It was Sister Mary Benedict, lips pursed and eyes squinty with disapproval.

He considered for a moment but no, it wouldn't have been proper. She wouldn't have read Lawrence and if she had she would have confessed and done absolution by now and wouldn't want to be reminded of it.

And that, he decided once again, really was the worst of it. There wasn't anyone to talk to. He could have taken it, all of it, the wheelchairs, the knitted caps, the twisted feet in their bedsocks, the ulcers, even the green-streaked sauce. But it was hard, having no one to talk to. That was hard.

'Sister,' he said, 'what are the chances of a pen and paper for me? My notebooks appear to be full . . .'

Because it had come to that at last, nothing but his thoughts and pen and paper; so who knew, perhaps now, at the end of his days, finally and in conclusion, there being absolutely nothing else for it, he might be able to write, he'd simply HAVE to write?

Or at the very least, begin to think seriously about what he was going to write. A memoir? His autobiography? He'd have to get his thoughts in line then, and that would give him something to think about.

He'd start with whatever came to mind, Rudy decided. The Salon, for instance, and himself sitting on a plank put across the leather arms of the huge old barber's chair for his first 'big boy's' haircut, watching the sharp pointed scissors snipping so fast and so finely that it was a wonder to behold: comb lifting the hair up, scissors lopping it off.

And after that playing around, conscious of the prickly feeling where his neck had been shaved, smelling the talcum powder which had sifted down inside his collar, slipping and sliding on the hair which had fallen on the lino-covered floor, sneaking sniffs at all the opaque bottles of oils, lotions and pomades. Later given a treat of a cooldrink in the small curtained-off back section where the kettle stood next to the gas-ring, together with the tins of tea and sugar and the mugs, mostly unwashed.

After he had learned to read he had pondered the legend: *WILMOT V. KNOESEN Professor of Tonsorial Artistics* scrolled above the doorway of the Salon, and been impressed by the lofty aspirations of his stepfather who was, after all, only an artisan, as he realised later, and hardly even well-read, unless the Reader's Digest counted for something.

He had been fond of music, though; he'd had a good voice and some talent, displayed annually at the eisteddfod when the Male Voice Choir went to compete. They had specialised in folk songs, sea shanties and the like, *Road to Mandalay*, *Waltzing Matilda*, and, he remembered, *Ikley Moor Baht 'At*, which his mother, originally from Yorkshire, had translated for him from the dialect, leaving him quite appalled at the thought of sinking below worms on the food chain and even more appalled at mankind's unwitting cannibalism.

He must have spent years of his life sitting in the back room of the Salon where they made tea on the gas-ring, in amongst the clutter of empty lotion and milk bottles and bowls of sugar lumpy with damp; where the towels were washed in the large sink by the silent black girl, to be hung out in the small yard behind the shop to dry.

He'd been intrigued by her. They spent so much time together, yet without ever saying a word beyond the basic 'hello', 'goodbye', 'excuse me', 'is there any tea?', 'the sugar-basin's empty', 'you'd better go and buy some more milk', etc.

She was stolid, accepting, always hanging over the sink of soapy water, rubbing, rinsing and wringing hundreds, possibly thousands of towels, ending the day with waterlogged hands, skin all rough, puffed and corrugated.

He'd asked her: 'Where's your home?' and she'd said: 'Patensie', which had meant nothing to him.

What else should he have asked?

'Are your parents alive?' 'What sort of life do you have?' 'Any leisure, hobbies, interests?' ' Husband?' 'Children?'

But her stolid silence had put him off, intimidated him to an extent. It would have been hard to penetrate the barrier she put up between herself and them, the master, the missus and the young master. They had belonged to different worlds, impinging on each other's only at places of mutual need — service and financial constraints.

The smells in the Salon had been as pervasive as those in the Home: perm lotions that irritated the mucous membranes of one's nose, the strong smell of the over-brewed tea in the buckled aluminium kettle, the acetone, nail polish, creams and powders, all overlaid with the smell of rubber from the heavy capes used to protect the customer's clothing from the all-but-corrosive perm lotions which could discolour beads and left dark brown stains on the towels; the stuff that could frizz hair into the tight little corkscrew curls that would defy comb and brush for months afterwards.

He'd seen it all in the Salon, the parade of fashion as the years and styles changed from the shingle to the Eton crop to the gamin; from the gentle finger waving to the tight little pincurls and sharply ridged waves made by the steel teeth of the goodie-grips, from the marcel waves steamed in with curling tongs to bangs and sweeps, page-boys, fringes and French rolls, at which point the Professor of Tonsorial Artistics had bowed out, to function henceforth in a supervisory role as the maestro, white-haired and venerable, adding his personal touch, the final tuck to every sleek head of hair until he had finally expired.

He, Rudy, had been a silent witness to it all, as silent as the 'girl' who washed the towels and seersucker capes used for cutting and setting. He'd sat there every afternoon after school, hunched on top of the stool at the back, staring at the counter in front of him, conscious of the homework in his book bag which he knew it would be a good idea to begin and get done with while he had nothing else to do, in order to be free later, when they'd all go home at last at around six o'clock in the evening, after his mother had cashed up, putting the day's takings in a bank bag in her handbag, and tidying up the 'reception', ready for the following day.

He'd have his lunch of viennas and chips or fish and chips or his sandwiches from Oelofse's (depending on how much they had in the till) and he'd sit, staring, thinking perhaps (but what had he had to think about, at his age?), his jaw relaxed and his overbite making him look like a little tortoise or a lizard (at least, that was what some of the children at school had said).

There were sounds as well as smells, he remembered. Only a curtain and a plywood partition had separated the back room from the rest of the Salon which was divided into small cubicles, also with painted plywood. He could hear his mother and stepfather and the other qualified assistant advising the customers, after listening to their troubles, their husbands' troubles and their children's troubles and he'd come to understand that there was a lot more to be gained from a visit to a Salon than simply having one's hair washed, permed and set, or one's nails manicured.

Hairdressers were like confessors. One could say things to one's hairdresser while she or he was turning up those myriad pincurls, that one couldn't tell anyone else, confident that it would never be repeated. One could expect counsel as well as the latest poodle-cut. He understood that hairdressers were the wisest of mortals. Troubles were spilled out over the manicuring table and advice was given that would have done a psychiatrist proud.

Oh yes, Rudy reflected, the Professor of Tonsorial Artistics could perhaps have considered himself a Professor of Psychology, and Sociology as well. He'd got the experience, if not the diplomas, to prove it.

He'd heard only snatches, of course, but it was enough, at least while he was young, to make him see his parents as influential and elevated, like the oracles of old; and indefatigable, with their brains, mouths and ears working as unceasingly as their nimble fingers; especially the Professor, on whose advice marriages were salvaged, or trashed, insight given into the behaviour of wayward and rebellious husbands and children, and financial advice dispensed, together with betting tips.

Horse-racing, Rudy had come to understand, was the only

18

topic more important than the many and varied family crises, especially around the time of the Durban July when everyone had had a tip from someone in the know and Rudy had been amazed to hear how much privileged information the Professor of Tonsorial Artistics had gleaned from who-knew-where since as far as Rudy knew, he divided his time between the Salon, home and the weekly choir practices.

'Dreams,' he had told Rudy once. 'The spirits tell me in dreams.'

'Nonsense,' his mother had said immediately and he had been inclined to agree with her, although it had been an intriguing thought, that heaven, or purgatory at least, should be peopled with pallid punters and horse-fanciers . . .

No wonder that both his mother and stepfather were so taciturn at day's end, with hardly a word to say to each other or to him. Having spent their long day listening to and advising so many people their supplies of wisdom and compassion were quite depleted by evening, and needing to be replenished by a good night's sleep, to be ready for the first sometimes tearful, sometimes cheerful, sometimes even slightly battered and bruised, clients the next morning.

He had discovered this during the holidays when he sometimes went with them to earn extra pocket-money by tidying the boxes of curlers and hairpins and distributing the combs and scissors retrieved from the small sterilising cabinet where they'd been kept overnight. The bruised and battered would be examined with 'oohs' and 'aahs' and 'shames' and 'bastard' by his mother and the assistant in a cubicle behind the drawn curtain.

It was like a hospital, he'd thought sometimes, or at least a clinic, where tea and sympathy and a brand-new hair-style, 'to give you a lift', was dispensed as therapy, plus advice to 'charge the bastard' of course.

He could often earn enough to go to the holiday shows at the Grand where there was a piano banging out *Happy Days Are Here Again* until the manager came onstage with his raucous 'Hi di hi' to lead them all in a ragged, screaming version of the song ending with a tremendous 'We're at the Grand there is no doubt!'

Tom Mix, Hopalong Cassidy, Roy Rogers and Trigger, Zorro, foreign legionaries and the pirates of Frenchman's Creek filled his lonely hours and he would enjoy, if only vicariously, a life of glamour, adventure and danger.

And now, he thought, the wheel had come full circle and he was back where he started, needing to fill the lonely hours, with the television a poor substitute for the silver screen, mingy little box that it was, miniaturising and trivialising everything, apart from being chronically out of focus.

He sat feeling sorry for himself, the more so because his jaw had suddenly clamped on his tongue in one of the strange muscle spasms he was experiencing from time to time, to leave a painful blood blister; spasms which affected his hands too, making them open involuntarily, without warning, so that he dropped whatever he was carrying.

Was it a sign of normal debilitation, he wondered, or was he developing some sort of degenerative nerve or muscle disease? Would the Sisters know?

The Professor of Tonsorial Artistics would have, he felt sure. He had known about such things. He'd gleaned them through a lifetime of devouring the Reader's Digest from cover to cover every month, together with such encyclopaedic compilations as *Household Medicine*, *Amateur Mechanics*, *Psychology for Everyman* etc, as the Digest had had on special offer once a year, a library Rudy had himself delved into until the time when he'd had the opportunity to savour the more sophisticated content of the widow Evadne's inherited collection.

Rudy was becoming increasingly aware of the strange hum which came from all sides and in waves. Impossible to describe, except in Afrikaans: *kerm en kou*. That's what it was. Complain and chew. Or whimper and whine, perhaps; a yammering, humming and hawing . . . They'd all do, as onomatopoeias went, but *kerm and kou* – that was the sound exactly. Twice a day it would intensify, to become really intrusive, a loud keening, an incessant nattering: 'kekekekenenenene' and 'aneeeaneeeakeeeakeee . . .'

For a while he had thought the noise was in his head, tinnitus or something, but when he asked Laetitia if she heard it too or if she thought it might be in his head, she said: 'Hokaaay . . .' considering the question carefully, which was why he liked her. She took him seriously; she didn't call him grandpa, or gramps, or oupa or even daddy any more. He had a thing about that, objecting because he had never been a grandfather, or even a daddy, his relationship with Lillith having been something quite other, and as nameless as any of Wilde's if the truth were told.

'Olraaaaait . . .' wobbling as she came over to speak into his good ear, her skirt undulating like a hula dancer's. 'It's the frail-care,' she told him. 'The very very frail-care in the beds, they only washing and drying them now, putting on a little bit of powder and cream, but they doan like it, but they must do it because of the sores and the piepie.'

'I was afraid it was my ears,' he told her.

'Maybe it's the wax,' she pronounced. 'Oanly wax, hokaaay?'

'Wax,' he agreed, taking her word for it.

'Yes mister. You thought what I must call you yet? If you doan like daddy?'

What indeed? He couldn't think for a moment. Imagine still having an identity crisis at seventy-five, or was it eighty? Imagine. As Lennon would have it.

'Colonel,' he said at last. 'You can call me Colonel.'

'You were a policeman, daddy, I mean Kernel?'

'A soldier,' he sighed. 'And tell them all, will you? Tell them to call me Colonel.' That was it. He was the Colonel. That's what it said on his nameplate, after all. He'd been 'Rudyard' to his teachers, 'Rude' to his friends, 'tortoise', 'skilpad' and 'lizard' to his enemies, 'RK' to Evadne and Lillith, 'the Colonel' to Annie, and 'Rudy' to Claude and company and to Mavis; but he chose to end his days as 'Colonel Knoesen'. He'd insist on it, on retaining something of his fast-fading dignity.

'And what causes the wax?' he wanted to know, wondering about all that sweet oil. Could it have congealed as it cooled down? Shouldn't his mother have known?

Laetitia screwed up her face and sneezed hard. She took snuff, he knew. He'd seen her sniffing and snorting and waving her hanky around in a sort of parody of Pavarotti – unconscious, of course, although she might have seen him on TV. It was altogether too prima donna-ish for Sister Mary Benedict, in any case, and Laetitia had been told to put the disgusting thing away and never to bring it out again.

'Olraait. The wax is when you get old, hokaaay?'

That was it then, he was becoming waxy on the inside. He was disintegrating, decaying, putrefying slowly, mouldering like a mushroom left out in the sun . . .

But that wasn't the most comforting line of thought to pursue. He'd have to get a grip on himself, pull himself together, forget the wax, the floaters in his eyes, his stiff joints and fingers and the spasms. He'd have to think about something else. Keep his brain going. There were too many brain-dead around there and he didn't want to become one of them. Not yet.

But what to think about? There was precious little in the way of intellectual stimulus around. Nothing but the wheelchair brigade in the passages, and the bleating bellyachers in the lounge . . .

It was fitting, Rudy thought, that having started life with nuns he should end with them. It was neat, coming full circle like that. Born in a Catholic nursing home, caught by a midwifing nun, schooled in a convent (as far as Standard Two anyway, after which the boys moved on to be educated by the Brothers, who were like the Sisters, his mother reassured him, only male).

His early most impressionable years then, were shaped by the stately sisters of the Assumption in their voluminous black habits, veils and tight white wimples, looking for all the world like large penguins. Covered from head to foot they'd been in those days, with only their pale soft hands and faces showing. Utterly mysterious and totally self-controlled.

The boys had done needlework with the girls, he remembered, none of the nuns having been able to teach woodwork; so there they had sat, too young to develop any sort of gender crisis (in any case alienation was a later invention, like the generation gap), learning to darn, to sew back-stitch and even, every other week, to knit.

It was good for them, Mother Superior had said. It taught them concentration and application, '. . . and don't you boys be turning your noses up at it. There's a fair career to be made at tailoring.'

Tailoring! All he knew about tailoring was what he had seen of the old Malay in his red fez and fluffy white beard sitting in his dark alleyway of a shop, day in and day out behind his huge black sewing machine, treadling endlessly, seam up and seam down, and nipping the threads off with his worn-down black stumps of teeth.

Had he ever seriously considered tailoring as a career? The alternative at that stage had been taking over the Salon and manning the huge steaming perm machine. He'd pictured himself behind both, with the sewing machine becoming a very ordinary contraption by comparison. He'd liked the old Malay's red fez, though, with its black tassel swinging jauntily at the side. Could he, as the Professor of Tonsorial Artistics' heir, have the best of both worlds and man the fearsome perm machine in a fez and tassel?

Rudy smiled to himself. Such innocence. Whatever had happened to it?

And now here he was, back with the nuns. A different order, of course, very different, post-Vatican II different, in their calf-length skirts and sandals, their hair showing at the edges of their headscarves. Rudy remembered how they had speculated about the nuns of the Assumption, giggling at the thought that their pates had to be bald as all get-out under those skin-tight wimples.

They were looking more human these days. Acting more human too, stomping around on their callouses, threatening the black staff with purgatory and worse.

Not that that bothered him. They all agreed the nuns had hearts of gold. They had to have. It would have been too terrifying otherwise, being aged and helpless and at their mercy.

They all tried to please the nuns anyway, just in case, and especially Mother Mary Therese, trooping in to mass, dousing themselves with holy water, while those who knew how to, assiduously counted the beads . . .

And what did it matter, after all; good thing to hedge one's bets as he'd always said, and especially now when they were all staring eternity in the face. Who knew what lay beyond? Not Rudy. For all he knew, the nether or supernal worlds – or both – might well be the celestial tote of the Professor of Tonsorial Artistics' dreams. He was willing to listen to any and all theories on the eternal verities and had even spent some time trying to engage Sister Mary Benedict in discussions on the subject.

Not that she ever had much time to actually discuss anything. She gave him the Catholic dogma which she knew by rote, as it behove her, through lips tightly pursed and admitting of no other possibilities.

He envied her. It had to be a good feeling, being so sure of oneself, of not having even the slightest doubt. He asked her once if she did or had ever doubted and she'd simply stared at him, presumably struck speechless at the thought.

Sister Mary Ambrose was just as doctrinaire. 'I'm Irish,' she'd said, as though that explained it all, and maybe it did.

Perhaps it would help, when the time came, that he had begun and was now ending his life in the company of those who were so confident?

Maybe, if he stayed there long enough (not that he had much choice in the matter) some of that assurance would rub off on him or be absorbed in a sort of mystic osmosis? One could only hope.

THREE

SIZING UP

ᕼ

'Faces like pickled bums,' Rudy's neighbour said. He hadn't got to know any of them yet, and the fact was, he wasn't sure that he wanted to from the look of some of them. But what was the alternative? Pretending that he was stone deaf, or still as catatonic as when they had pulled him in? He'd carefully control all social intercourse, he decided, until he'd had a chance to size them up. No bores, he thought. He'd be like Byron.

'Pardon?' he said, turning his head to present his good ear.

'I said, faces like pickled bums.'

It was true of course, at least of the plump ones. 'Bums like pickled bums too, I'll bet.'

'Bums like pickled bums,' the old man chortled, banging his walking stick on the floor a few times, to show his appreciation, Rudy supposed.

'Better anyway, I think.'

'Better what?'

'The thin ones. All bones and blather. McNaughton,' he said. 'Neville McNaughton.'

Rudy shook the large knobbly hand stretched out to him.

'Knoesen,' he said.

'I know. The Colonel. Seen action myself, you know. North Africa. Middle East. Get as far as that? Bahrain. Regular wringer of a place. Regular bloody hothouse. Heat like a presence, most days.'

Should he try to dredge up something about the Legion, Rudy wondered. But what? Neville McNaughton may have seen the Colman films as well.

'Especially that one,' Neville said, pointing with his stick at one of the old women who was sitting with her thin legs splayed to accommodate a small table on which she had laid out rows of playing cards.

'That one what?' Rudy asked.

'That one especially. All bones and blather. Tell your future for you. Sees it in the cards.'

'Future? Even I could tell my future,' Rudy said. 'There isn't one, not to speak of, and I don't need cards for that.'

The old woman leaned over, her small dark eyes rolling like marbles in her head, the loose folds of flesh hanging down from her arms quivering as she shuffled, dealt, gathered up and shuffled again. 'Your fortune,' she said. 'Don't you want to hear your fortune?'

Rudy stared at her, wondering who she reminded him of, and then it came back in a flash: the tearoom on the terrace, the small tables draped in white damask, the waitresses in their black dresses, frilly white aprons and caps and the elderly pianist with her hair in sharply ridged waves, sitting just so, legs splayed, sharp elbows held out, her magenta velvet gown pulled up, her bony knees pumping away at the pedals, her spindly fingers shuffling over the keys while the extremely refined, angular lady with the reedy voice sang pointedly, he thought: *I'm a rowdy dowdy that's me . . .* although he'd done his best, he remembered, going so far as to wear pumps and spats . . .

He saw it all again, the images evoked by the old fortune-teller, with her equally sharply angled knees and elbows straddling her card-table like a spider.

He'd proposed to Evadne right there in that tearoom while the chanteuse trilled: '*She's a high-hat baby that's she . . .*' trying not to be put off by Evadne's sharp birdlike features, her heavily powdered cheeks, the exaggeratedly high pencilled arches over the imperfectly plucked natural line of her eyebrows.

He hadn't liked the look of her from the very beginning, so while he proposed he had concentrated on her jaunty little yellow hat with the yellow feathers fanning out above it. That, and the white dress she wore, made her look like a cockatiel. Cockatiel from hell, as it turned out . . .

'Going to do physio?' Neville McNaughton asked.

'No,' Rudy said. 'Shouldn't think so.' It had depressed him, the memory of Evadne, and that fateful day in the tearoom.

Because if he hadn't married her he wouldn't have become involved with Lillith, and if he hadn't become involved with Lillith, he wouldn't have been caught at the old slap and tickle. *In flagrante delicto*. What did that mean exactly? Delectably flagrant? Flagrantly delectable? Aye, he thought. That it was and all.

He heaved a great pained sigh at the memory of Lillith, little giggling Lillith. Only she'd giggled him right into jail, she had . . .

'It's compulsory,' Neville McNaughton informed him. 'Unless you've got a dicky heart.'

'What is?' Rudy came back with a start.

'The physio. You've got to do it.'

'I know what compulsory means,' Rudy grumped. They all grumped. He'd got into the habit in no time at all. 'What for anyway?'

'Circulation. It's good for the circulation. Keep the old ticker pumping. Otherwise . . .' he thumped his walking stick on the floor, hinting at something dire, Rudy supposed.

'Stop banging like that, Mac,' one of the pickled bum faces complained. 'And I wouldn't mind a reading, Mrs Myles, if you can spare the time.'

The angular fortune-teller shuffled, elbows windmilling around. 'If you don't do physio,' she informed Rudy, 'you'll get a clot and gangrene and end up in a wheelchair. I can tell you that for nothing.'

'In the cards, is it? Or ON the cards, I suppose . . .' Rudy smiled.

Sister Mary Ambrose came in with a huge vase of poinsettias which she put down on the table in the middle of the room. There was an immediate buzz as they all took note.

'Ohhhhh, nice . . .'

'Where do THEY come from?'

'Don't they just brighten the place up?'

The only other old man in the room left his chair on the far side to join Rudy and Neville McNaughton. He had a big backside and walked with a distinct sway of the hips. Rheumatism, Rudy thought, arthritis maybe, or just plain womanish?

'Puts me in mind of the Lowveld,' he said. 'Lived there, you know. God's own country.'

Sister Mary Ambrose looked at him over her rimless spectacles. 'You've not been to Ireland, then,' she said.

'God's own country,' the old man insisted. 'But hot. Like a hothouse in summer. Still and all, it got the poinsettias growing, real poinsettias, not scraggly like these. Singles and doubles. Not to mention the bougainvillea. Or the flamboyants, like gigantic bouquets all along the road.'

'Hot!' Neville McNaughton snorted, banging his walking stick. 'You want to try Bahrain. Forty-five, fifty degrees. Hits you on the head like a mallet. Here. Have you met Colonel Knoesen? Hargood,' Neville introduced them.

'Lyle,' the old man said, lifting his hand in a flutter of greeting. 'Dry with it, though, except when a thunderstorm was brewing, then there'd be all that moisture in the air.'

'Moist and misty and green, God's own country,' Sister Mary Ambrose countered. 'That's Ireland.'

The old woman on Rudy's right leaned over suddenly to grab his arm, her eyes wild above her pudgy cheeks. 'That day, did I tell you?' she hissed. 'That day was so bad I hid behind the bed because we had to go and see Alistair who had gone so thin he looked ninety, even the whites of his eyes . . .'

'What?' Rudy asked in some alarm.

'Always been full of himself, but he hides things. Wait until he gets tired of the game and then it will all come out. Like what he was doing in the park. Ask him what he was doing in the park . . .'

Rudy shook himself free. 'Who? Mr Hargood? Lyle?'

'ALISTAIR!' she shrieked.

Sister Mary Ambrose was the only one in the room, apart from Rudy, who reacted. 'Shhhhh . . .' she said, putting a soft white finger to her lips. 'Don't take on so.'

'Star of India,' Lyle Hargood said wistfully. 'And the pink kapoks . . . Stick a twig of bougainvillea in and there'd be the new growth, starting at the little nodes. Take over a whole tree, like a garland. . .'

'Sandy bloody place,' Neville McNaughton offered. 'Nothing there.'

'What do you mean, nothing there? We ran a nursery, Mother and me . . .'

'BAHRAIN!' Neville thumped on the floor. 'Talking about the DESERT!'

'You're the only one then,' Lyle grumped, going back to his

chair.

The physiotherapist arrived and began to fiddle with her cassette player, going backwards and forwards until she had what she wanted, a stirring bit of martial music, the beat very regular and pronounced.

Under forty, Rudy noticed at once. And not too bad either, although her hair was a bit greasy, especially at the roots.

'Good morning!' she said brightly. 'And how are you all today? On your feet, please, no excuses, no trouble now!'

Grumbling, those who weren't in wheelchairs heaved themselves up.

'One, two, three, begin! Right arm up, round and down, left arm up, swing across and down . . .' she called out.

They ranged around her in a circle but their response was half-hearted, their movements perfunctory, hardly more than a hand lazily raised and waved.

'Right leg UP, and DOWN . . . Shoulders up and dr. . .OP! Left leg up!'

Mrs Myles lifted her leg and knocked her little table over, sending the cards flying. 'Drat!' she said. 'There goes your fortune, Joey.'

'I'LL be gone in a minute,' Joey wheezed, 'never mind my fortune . . .'

'Left foot, one step OUT, right foot . . .'

That was too much for most of them. Those who were still trying were getting it all wrong anyway, heels in when they should have been out, until one after the other, huffing and puffing, they gave up and sank back into their chairs.

'And that's going to stop the clots?' Rudy asked Lyle who had taken a chair next to his.

'She's sharp, that one,' Lyle confided. 'No flies on her.'

Rudy stared at the physiotherapist with some interest. 'Sharp, is she?' Pity that she was so ordinary looking then; no make-up, greasy hair, shapeless legs . . .

'Knees UP . . .' she coaxed those who were still standing. 'Right knee UP!'

Rudy stayed down, but he lifted one foot after the other to please her. Might be worth cultivating, he thought. Right side of forty at least. That counted for something.

'And re. . .EST!' the physiotherapist trilled as the thumpity thump came to an end.

'Water,' one of the pickled bums gasped. 'My mouth's that dry.'

'Try shutting up then,' Neville grumped.

'Not like Mauritius, perhaps, or Hawaii,' Lyle mused, 'but still lush, profuse, anything grows, any excuse to . . .'

The old woman on the other side of him clutched Rudy's arm again. 'Excuse? You just ask him what he was doing out there behind the tree in the park. No consideration for the rest of us, not him. No excuse for that! Dirty old man!'

'Alistair?' Rudy asked.

'DOUG!' she yelled. 'Douglas! Douggie!'

'Nothing but rotting vegetation and BUGS!' Neville McNaughton glowered. 'It's the desert for me, if you want to know . . .'

All right, Rudy decided. It wasn't too bad, now that he was getting to know some of them. Conversation of a sort was possible. Better than nothing, anyway.

'What about this place, the Eastern Cape?' he asked.

'Well, what about it?'

'Not so lush, perhaps, but did you know that the first horse races in the country were run here? Back in the 1880s . . .'

'Horses!' Neville snorted. 'This is donkey country, mate. Mule at a stretch.'

Rudy felt slighted. Strange how one tended to identify with the place of one's birth and nurturing.

'Grahamstown's quite pretty,' Lyle offered.

'This place has always been a no-starter,' Neville said, jabbing viciously at the floor with his stick. 'If you're talking horses you're flogging a dead one.'

'And I'm afraid the vegetation . . .' Lyle began doubtfully.

'All right,' Rudy conceded. It wasn't the Lowveld. Or Ireland. Endless tracts of aloe and prickly pear, that was all. Of no use apart from providing bedrock for rail and road to take the traveller to other, more attractive regions . . .

'And the wind . . .' Lyle said.

'Bloody black south easter! Give you sinus, hay fever, asthma, TB . . .'

Probably true, Rudy thought. He couldn't make any sort of a case for the place, but still, he loved it. He loved it as one tended to love a handicapped child or the runt of a litter. It was home. It was where he had started out and it was where he was expecting to see his end. Right there, in the Home, in the tatty old heart of the city.

Sister Mary Ambrose had very kindly given him a cheap ballpoint and a nearly new lined blue writing pad. Not too conducive, he'd thought. Not as conducive as the gold Crosses and Schaeffers and reams of stylish writing paper, creamy-white and subtly textured, which Evadne's late husband, the Dean, had left her.

But it was better than nothing.

He sat on his bed, willing the ideas to come bubbling up, and was suddenly reminded of Annie. They had been reading Proust together and she was encouraging him to start writing his own memoir. He could almost hear her pleading with him:

'Pretend it's a letter to me. Just start "Dear . . ." But perhaps you wouldn't start "Dear"?' She'd laughed her diffident, self-deprecating little laugh,' and when he hadn't laughed, she'd stopped, embarrassed, which he hadn't meant her to be. She'd been too sensitive by far. A bit of a strain sometimes.

'Odd way to start a memoir,' he'd said. 'But of course, "Dear". Dear Annie. What else?'

She'd appeared mollified, and the devil of it was, he'd more than half meant it, he really had . . . Dear Annie.

'Just start at the beginning,' she'd said. 'Anything and everything. Thoughts, dreams, impressions . . .'

She'd made it sound so easy. She'd never understood how difficult it was for him to get anything down on paper, especially something about himself, like a memoir, which had at least to touch on the truth. Because it hardly bore repeating, the truth about his life, not even touches of it.

Nothing worth writing about, anyway. Nothing that would stand the test of time, ring down through the ages, resonate, change lives . . . A brief tinkle, perhaps, as of a little breeze just brushing chimes on a front porch. Barely there before it would be gone, with hardly a vibration remaining. *'Did I hear something just now?' 'A faint tinkle, you mean? Oh, that was just his life, Rudy's, R K Knoesen's, the Colonel's. The old dissembler's . . .'*

What did he remember about his life, in any case? Only patches of memory left, the rest short-circuited by the ECTs. Or wiped out by Time, the Great Eraser. No continuity any more. Just a hop, skip and jump from one thing to another.

Like now, back to Annie and that day, sitting out in the sun which was hot and white, having passed its apex about an hour previously, her hair glinting red and gold, her neck long and white and thickish. Very art nouveau. Weirdsley Beardsley, as she used to say.

'Not nearly patrician enough, my antecedents,' he'd said. 'Nothing like Proust's.'

She'd looked so disappointed that he'd relented: 'All right. We'll start with a quotation. That's an elegant way to start a memoir.'

'*Intellect distinguishes between the possible and the impossible . . .*' he began. He had a good hand, Rudy knew. Everyone said so and he was proud of it. Verging on copperplate, or would have if he'd had a better pen.

'And start with the present. This place,' she'd said. 'The place of our present pain.'

That place. Not pain so much as complete debilitating boredom, he thought, at least until the day Annie had arrived. He'd put a warped LP on the wobbly record-player and asked her to dance. She'd been completely disoriented and dishevelled, her cheeky little beret quite skew, but oh, how they'd danced! Buckling this way and that, singing along: . . . *bluer than velvet was the night* . . .' which had been apposite enough, considering the fuzz the chemical cocktail had put on everything, muffling thought and emotion as under a deep velvet pile.

She had been crying but she'd stopped by then. It must have been just too distracting, that hip-wrenching tango. *Rose in Spanish Harlem*, he remembered. Stirring song. Striking girl.

Much later he'd asked her about relationships, liaisons. She might have been married for all he knew, might have had a husband lurking around somewhere; estranged, perhaps, but she'd still not have been free . . . Not that he had had designs of that sort, any more than he'd had divorce papers; unless Evadne had divorced him after all. But how would he have known unless he'd gone digging through the whole sordid mess again?

She'd been embarrassed. 'Not me,' she'd said. 'No one's ever thought that way about me.'

Poor Annie. Always putting herself down.

Not too difficult either, when she WAS down, in the depths of the deepest depression he had ever seen (apart from those who cocooned themselves in their sheets and turned their faces to the wall). It had been one or the other with Annie, as the pendulum swung: listless and morbid, or on a self-generating high, neurons transmitting like an express train fuelled, the Shaman had told him, by noradrenalin.

He'd done what he could for her, comforted, encouraged her; but she hadn't been all that receptive, as he remembered. Not that he could, or did, blame her . . .

The devil of it was, he'd really been attracted, especially that day in the little yard behind the Centre, sitting in the sun on the stone bench, in amongst the weeds, broken bottles, half-bricks and plastic bags, discussing his projected memoir. He'd wanted to throw caution to the winds, to say: 'Let's make love, Annie, here on the bench, right now, you and I, with the sun to warm my bare bot and . . .'

Sheer madness of course, even to think of such a thing. That midsummer dream of a day must have gone to his head.

Rudy looked around and realised with some relief that it was tea-time, or coffee-time, since there was a choice in the afternoons. Coffee then, and a rusk like a shard of granite to dunk and suck on. Something, anyway, to take his mind off what they'd had for lunch: mince swimming in khaki juice, Sister Mary Bartholomew's version of bobotie.

'We can't make the curry too strong, Colonel,' she'd told him, 'for those with hiatus hernia.' She'd stood, four-square solid, beads of perspiration glistening on her moustache and eyebrow – she only had one, usually drawn up in a fearful frown – holding her wooden ladle like a sceptre, looking for all the world like Rackham's squat Queen of Hearts. And why not? She was queen of the kitchen, after all, with decisions regarding curry powder her absolute, royal prerogative . . .

Idle to speculate after the event, but if he hadn't been married (or supposing he had known for sure that Evadne had divorced him), would he have proposed to Annie?

No point in even thinking about it, of course. The fact was, he had proposed to Evadne and he was probably still married to the woman.

She'd accepted him with quite a few simpers and sighs that fateful day in the tea-room and a day or two later he'd gone around to her house to confirm or consolidate, if not consummate, the thing.

It had been raining hard, he remembered, and all she had to wear (or so she said) was a monogrammed handtowel which she'd draped around herself, unaware perhaps that it did not quite cover her bottom, which had dropped, and her thighs, which were pocked with cellulite.

'Very South Seas I'm sure,' he'd managed to say lightly. 'You make me feel like Gauguin . . .' Only he'd said 'Gorgon', his knowledge of art having been gleaned from the Digest, which didn't provide the phonetics.

She'd laughed at him. 'What's that?' she asked. 'A gargoyle? Gorgon the gargoyle?'

Still, they'd enjoyed some smoked salmon and Mozart together before he dropped the stones in her lap (she'd found a kimono, 'just barely dry', by then) saying: 'Get them set any way you like,' as cavalier as Fairbanks or Flynn.

Looking back on it now he was glad they had only been cubic zirconia.

Evadne had wanted to wear her grandmother's wedding dress, which was in the way of being a family heirloom, kept in her grandfather's cello case which stood like a sarcophagus in a corner of the hall, *sans* cello, and containing only the old wedding dress, sere and crinkly like paper, its sleeves with their tiny buttons going right up to the elbows neatly folded across the bodice, overlaid with bits and pieces of wire and net, all that was left of the bouquet which must have trailed right down to the floor. Ceremoniously incarcerated. Laid to rest, as it were.

But since she'd already worn it once, many years ago, when she'd married the late Dean, then a junior lecturer, she'd decided on something 'more stylish' instead.

The wedding itself had been the stuff of nightmares: the chapel like a mausoleum, a hundred years old at least, the priest a nodding death's head, intoning the marriage office as if it were the last rites – which in a way it had been – the choristers draped in long white shrouds; Evadne's sister, gaunt as a skeleton; her mother, superannuated to the point of mummification; her nieces, Rowena, Edwina and Philippa, wraithlike in their wispy gowns, and Evadne. Evadne the widow, the bride, in a diaphanous grey creation like the layers of a spider's web.

Only Lillith had looked as if she still belonged to the land of the living. As for himself, he felt at that moment that he had left it for ever.

He hadn't, of course. He'd lived with Evadne, watching her become more and more pretentious, modelling herself on the dangle-earringed dilettantes on the fringes of the art world, always going to paint, write, sculpt, compose . . . but all she had ever done was draw, scribble, dabble and tinkle on the piano. She'd swanned around in convulsively coloured smocks with peaked turban-like 'ethnic' contraptions on her head which made her look like a woodpecker, and *La Nausée* under her arm. In the original, although her French had never been that good.

She'd probably married him thinking that he would be bound to succeed as a writer, and at that stage he had been quite hopeful himself. They hadn't discussed it, of course. They'd been pretty taciturn with each other; and the more so as time passed.

Still, Evadne did have one notable accomplishment, as it turned out. Two, in fact: she could make a tomato soup so thick and rich that it made the perspiration break out on his forehead, and a lemon pudding so tart and sweet at the same time that it crimped the palate and brought tears to the eyes.

The highlights of his marriage. No more than culinary, to be sure, but highlights for all that, and better than nothing.

His own mother hadn't lived to see the wedding. Poor woman, with her amorphous features, calico-coloured skin and eyes like small dark buttons, she'd come to resemble a ragdoll, especially after the Professor of Tonsorial Artistics had scorched her hair into a frizz.

Rudy remembered how afraid he had been the first time he'd seen her hooked up to the steaming machine with its long dangly wires and metal clips hissing, sizzling and singeing as they connected with the tightly rolled up sections of hair to make crisp little sausages all over her head.

He'd held her hand anxiously throughout the whole procedure, fearful that her head and face would be carbonised before his very eyes. There had been something infernal about it, the spluttering steam and the smell of burnt hair, something outlandish, like a scene in a science fiction movie. Indeed, wired up to it, her amorphous pudding of a face flushed beneath it, his mother had looked like an alien, something from the outer or even the nether world. He'd really been afraid: WAS it his mother, or had she undergone a Kafkaesque metamorphosis into a strange robot-like being powered by the great round metal ring of the fearsome perm machine?

She'd worn spectacles, his mother, rimless bifocals like Sister Mary Ambrose, which clipped her nose tightly at the bridge, leaving deep red indents on either side, as he saw when she removed them to go under the machine, making her seem even more alien and unlike herself.

Those were his abiding impressions.

For the rest her personality was as undefined as her face and his stepfather had dominated them both. He had been tall and dapper with dark curly eyelashes and a soft pink mouth. 'A real rosebud of a mouth,' his mother used to say, 'like Valentino's, or Navarro's.' And later, when he was old enough to go to the movies himself he saw that his stepfather had indeed modelled himself on the old matinée idols, with his pencil-thin black moustache (touched up, as he himself had seen, with his mother's Maybelline), his heavily brilliantined hair and mathematically precise centre parting.

He'd often wondered about his mother and her nondescript life; indeed, the nondescript lives of so many others of their acquaintance. They came, achieved nothing and nothing marked their passing. They made no mark of any sort and left nothing but children.

Had his mother ever wondered what her life had been about? Why she had been born to endure a short and unhappy first relationship – of which he, Rudy, had been the sole product – and then endure the second match to the handsome hairdresser, content to simply work, eat and sleep. Had she expected more from life?

She had, after all, been quite good-looking in her youth, judging from the old photograph she'd shown him. She'd had a good figure, fashionably slim in her ankle-length, softly draped dress – bias cut, which had flattered her hips but not her little round stomach – with the pointed lace-up shoes, a fox fur draped casually over one shoulder, gloved, and with a clutch bag resting in the crook of her elbow. A cloche hat framed the plaits coiled neatly around her ears. Her hair had been reddish-brown, almost auburn, she'd told him, before the perm lotions had bleached it to the colour of straw.

She'd looked a bit like the Duchess of Windsor then, elegant and emaciated, before the greasy doughnuts and other pastries she had favoured had rounded her features and figure until she'd ended with the lumpy, stuffed body and amorphous features of a ragdoll.

He, Rudy, was her only legacy, achievement even, and for a long time he had felt the burden of that, feeling that he'd have to achieve something for both of them, to justify their existences, hers and his.

Not that she had ever put such an onus on him. She'd never required anything from him, really, or if she'd had expectations she'd kept them to herself as she did most of her feelings.

There had been few intimate moments between them, and no real warmth. She'd never touched him apart from a brief kiss to say hello and goodbye and she'd stopped doing that when he turned ten. She'd have liked a daughter, he'd heard her say, a companion, someone to go shopping and have tea with.

Not that she'd ever resented him for not having been that daughter. Her whole attitude was one of passive acceptance of her lot. He hadn't even been able to make her angry. Punishment, like approval, was measured out in a totally mechanical way. His mother only went through the motions of living, he'd often thought. Or she lived her life vicariously, having found the experiences of her clients in the Salon so much more real and exciting than her own.

What could have happened to her? In an effort to understand he'd studied her photo album, hoping to discover some clue as to her antecedents and therefore his. She'd declined to comment on anything. 'Old pictures,' she'd said, terse as always. 'Just the family. Nothing much to tell.' And he'd had to leave it at that. His mother's family were nameless, his relatives were strangers: ladies in turbans and dungarees grouped around old Austins and Anglias, sitting on windswept pebbly beaches, sandwiches in hand, or snapped by photographers as they walked down unfamiliar city streets . . .

'Bolton,' she'd said, and 'Blackburn', and what did that mean to him?

Something must have happened to estrange her so completely from her own family. Something serious. Like expecting an illegitimate baby? Namely himself? Serious enough in those days. But she would never have told him, and he could never have asked. Later though, he did discover at least one reason for her chronic defeatism: the Professor of Tonsorial Artistics 'played around', as he'd overheard his mother tell one of her clients. Rudy knew that he played the horses but he gathered instinctively that 'playing around' meant having a flutter of a different sort. He never asked for details. The hurt and bitterness in his mother's voice distressed him so much that he didn't want to know any more about it.

What sort of relationship had they had then, his acquiescent mother and charming stepfather, the bogus Professor, always so devoted in the Salon? If they'd been inclined to answer, he had often thought, his stepfather would have said 'convenient' and his mother 'bogus'.

Years later he'd found another photograph in a box hidden behind the nightclothes and spencers in his mother's cupboard, a very old photograph taken by one Arthur Debenham, a 'Photographer and Miniature Painter' residing at 69 Palmerston Road, Bolton, dated July 1907. The establishment was 'under royal patronage' and the customer was also informed that the negative 'is preserved for future copies, enlargements or miniatures'.

The photograph itself depicted a very solemn young lady, her thick brown plaits secured on top of her head, the effect softened by shorter curls above the brow. She was gazing away over her right shoulder and her profile, Rudy thought, was very patrician indeed, very classical. Roman, in fact, the nose straight and prominent, the eyes large and wide, the mouth small and perfectly formed.

She wore a pearl choker and very pretty wide lace ruffles framed the top of her dress. And above the rather low-cut square neckline, another lace surround, gathered up with a narrow ribbon, appeared to have been added later for modesty's sake.

Who had she been? Part of his mother's family, obviously. Judging by the date, an aunt, or even her own mother, his grandmother? Her photograph kept hidden all those years, in any case, and she herself never mentioned, not to him anyway.

There was also – amongst the paraphernalia of old birthday cards, wedding invitations and suchlike, a slim, badly foxed volume of verse and essays, bound in soft cloth, like a child's book, without imprimatur of any sort.

Privately printed, he surmised, by the essayist, 'Aurelia', whoever she may have been, and impossible now to discover, especially if it were a *nom de plume*.

The booklet fell open where a fringed leather marker must have been placed many years before, at a poem written by someone called 'Delius'. A child, he thought, or a young person at least, since its execution was a trifle awkward.

From hot to cold, light to dark
Glad sunshine to shaded, shadow'd park
A wooded hill plunging down, down
In a maddening mill of gnarled trees,
Decaying leaves, to a (foxed) *stream*
And on the crown, a darkling ruin . . .

Darkling. Now there was a word to conjure with. Rudy was glad it hadn't got foxed.

He had read it all, hoping to discover some clue as to the identity of the authors. But there was nothing. One could only surmise. Mother and son, perhaps? Had the mysterious young woman captured in all her regal solemnity by the photographer, Debenham, been 'Aurelia'? Could she have become his paternal grandmother and 'Delius' his father?

He hoped so. Because then he would have been born into a literary tradition of sorts, albeit a tenuous one, since that slim, cloth-bound volume was all the evidence of it that he had ever been able to discover.

The fact was, he'd been able to discover precious little about himself. With a name like Rudyard Kipling, who could his father have been? A relative of THE Rudyard? Another raffish soldier/poet? A rabid colonialist? One of the old Empire-builders?

His mother would tell him nothing, not even on her death-bed. She was Mrs Knoesen and he, Rudy, had been duly adopted, and that was the end of it.

Rudyard Kipling Knoesen. With a name that coupled Boer and Brit it was no wonder that he'd been prey throughout his life to conflict and confusion, unresolved and unremitting.

FOUR

DRIBBLING ON

He'd been in the Home for quite a few months before – like the first day of spring itself – two student nurses appeared.

They were doing their practicals in geriatrics, they said, giggling and blushing, their tunics just above their pink dimpled knees, their hair soft and feathery.

'Come and do me then,' he'd invited. 'I'm geriatric, if anything. Come,' he'd coaxed, spreading his legs and patting his knees, 'one for each of you. For your practicals. And mine.'

But they'd giggled and declined. 'Too bony', they'd said. 'By half', and 'We don't trust you.'

The exchange had given him a bit of a rush. Strange how some things never faded, like some memories . . . of small soft bottoms spreading themselves over one's thigh and knee . . . Or was he only imagining things? Because after all, there hadn't ever been any ballerinas in their tight little tutus. That had been wishful thinking. What there HAD been was Lillith, before the rot had set in.

It had started, he remembered, with her jumping out from the shadows of the stairwell behind the settle to frighten him.

She'd been too old for that game, but she'd played it again and again, coming out to drop, as if exhausted, on to the settle until he'd joined her there, also feigning exhaustion (odd how he'd feigned things most of his life; hadn't he ever been genuine about anything?).

She'd eased herself on to his lap soon enough and they'd sit while he removed her shoes and her socks and began to tickle her little pink toes.

Toes were an erotogenic zone for him, he'd discovered; and perhaps for her also, considering her squeals and squirms (or had it been the squeals and squirms which had aroused him so?). It had all been part and parcel, anyway.

Part and parcel of his youth, or at least his young manhood, and it didn't bear thinking about, considering the outcome. So he thought instead of his mother's youth and what she may have been like before she'd become addicted to doughnuts and bloated and metamorphosed into a ragdoll.

She used to sing songs that must have brought back memories (none of them shared with him of course):

. . . ten pretty girls in the village school . . .

She couldn't have been one of them, he didn't think; then again, judging from another of the old photographs he had found, in her tam-o'-shanter and blazer buttoned across her slim hips, her short skirt and long shapely legs, she might just have made the list, at seventeen or so.

There was also that sideways glance, taunting, and the twinkle in the eye, approaching a gleam, actually, of pure mischief, so she must have been a bit of a tease. His mother. Imagine that . . .

And the Professor of Tonsorial Artistics? Rudy knew nothing about HIS youth, he having been a bit past it when he'd married his mother (widowed by then, or so she'd told everyone).

But in the early days he hadn't been at all bad looking,

46

Rudy thought, seeing him again on one of their family holidays in the Hogsback, sitting in lordly solitude, drinking his Pimm's No 1 Cup to cool down after the slogs in the forest.

He'd introduced himself to everyone as a Professor of Tonsorial Artistics, the last words spoken in an unintelligible mumble, and, having taken them all in, he'd spent the rest of the time looking erudite, as befitted a Professor of some obscure discipline, and been accorded the deference due to a gentleman of his academic standing, since no one had had the gumption to ask straight out: 'Professor of what did you say?'

When the Professor had finally passed on, Rudy and his mother had had to remove to a boarding-house in South End.

Rudy remembered the magnificent view they had had, of the bay and the patchwork of multicoloured roofs in between, pitched roofs, gabled roofs, flat roofs, tilted roofs, some with rickety wooden balconies festooned with the family laundry – mainly nappies – which the Indian women in their brilliant saris tended, conducting their conversations from one balcony or window to the next, two or three down, and even across the street.

One could walk to the beach from there, along the narrow old streets with their crumbling semi-detached houses.

It had been a densely populated area, 'mixed' in those days, full of colour and vitality, but designated a slum by the authorities, due for expropriation and clearance under the Group Areas Act.

A shame, he had often thought, and sometimes, a scandal; especially after eating a take-away curry from GeeDee's, the best café in town; but like all the rest, doomed to demolition.

They said the area wasn't safe, but since he didn't ever venture too far into the crooked alleys and dank backstreets, he didn't know.

He'd even had a few girlfriends there (of questionable ethnic origin, it had to be admitted) whom he'd taken to GeeDee's when he was flush, and when he wasn't, he'd taken them to the museum, the old museum in Bird Street, to peer into the glass-fronted display cabinets at all sorts of oddities, mammalian and reptilian, feigning interest for the girl's sake, the main purpose having been to walk hand in hand, to stand behind her with his arms around her pliant waist, while he moved up against the cleft of her behind; unobtrusively of course, more a gentle pressure than a rub, really, at the same time distracting her with sardonic comments on the poor stuffed animals' glass eyes, moth-eaten coats and withered paws. . .

Which brought him back to the present and the museum pieces THEY had all become with their glassy eyes, threadbare clothes and clawlike hands. Arthritis, gout, they had it all, every joint-crippling, limb-twisting condition there was, and unlike the dassies and meercats in the museum, they were all still alive, although just barely so.

But worse than the physical deformities were the mental incapacities and decrepitude.

It was bedlam. Rudy sometimes thought he was the only sane person there. Apart from the physiotherapist, perhaps. No flies on her, Lyle Hargood had said. What had he meant by that? That one could expect some sort of intelligent exchange from her? Would it be worth a try? Unattractive little thing, though, lank greasy hair, pale face. Might have been made a bit more presentable with a perm, perhaps. Not the singed frizzes the Professor of Tonsorial Artistics had specialised in, but one of the new perms, cold perms they called them, much more natural-looking. That, and a touch of colour to her lips, her cheeks, only just perceptible, subtle, the way they did everything these days.

The beauty business had become much more sophisticated, no doubt about it. None of that dead-white powder, those exaggerated blood-red bow-lips, plucked eyebrows and thin pencilled arches above. All the rage when he was young, of course. Strange how the perception of beauty had changed. They had shapes these days, in spite of all the bra burning, natural shapes, instead of flat-as-a-board-boyish the way they used to be, had to be, if they wanted to wear those flowing bias-cut dresses. Had to be pretty flat or they'd look like balloons, material straining in all directions.

And natural, shining hair too, blowing free, none of those old tortured corkscrew curls and ridged waves. Blow-dry they called it, and that was what they looked like, the curls, blowing around like bubbles in the wind . . .

The physiotherapist needed something like that. Because the potential was there, no doubt about it. And if, as Lyle Hargood had said, there were no flies on her . . . No wedding-ring either, he'd noticed, or engagement ring, or any kind of a ring . . .

But was she cultured? Articulate? Creative? Unlikely, considering her particular line of work. Still, could he justifiably call himself creative? On the evidence of his one novel and other bits and pieces, consisting mainly of notes written to himself, encouraging himself to write?

Some of them rather nice and evocative though, if his memory served him, which was moot, these days. All unfinished in any case, apart from the one novel which he had finished, using the late Dean's portable, and delivered hot off the platen as it were, not even stopping to wash his carbon-stained fingers. And where had THAT got him?

Better to leave the rest as they were. They provided him with a *raison d'être*, in a way. He'd kept himself going for years by the simple expedient of never finishing anything. His little rat's nest of notes tucked away in the black notebooks gave him a warm sense of a secret life, of having something no one else knew about, the way a hen might feel about her hidden clutch of unhatched eggs.

And now, considering the relentless nature of time, when it might be argued that if he was going to share his life's work, inconclusive as it was, he had better get on with it, there was no one to share it with. He'd missed his chances with Annie, always putting her off, indulging in all sorts of subterfuges and evasions. And Mavis wouldn't have been impressed, any more than Zolah would. Might have used them to stoke the outside boiler, if she'd known about them.

He'd reached the tail-end of his life, with his complete *oeuvre* still squirrelled away, and no one remotely interested.

He might try the physiotherapist; although he could imagine the exchange: 'Listen up, if you don't mind. I've written a little piece.'

'A little piece of what?'

'A little piece of writing. What else?'

He wasn't too hopeful. Whatever Lyle might think, she had struck him as being on the obtuse side.

And so here he was, at the dog-end of his days with his few pitiful pieces in the four black notebooks, carried around like a penance in the scuffed leather suitcase . . .

From memory, though (and of course memory can be deceptively self-indulgent), some of the pieces flowed quite nicely, with an effortless, artless unfolding. Not quite Rushdie, perhaps, but not as chokingly controlled and inhibited as his earlier stuff had been either; his one novel for instance . . .

And now there it all was. His life's work, the distillation of his entire thought and experience, buried under disintegrating socks and sagging underpants in a nicked leather suitcase.

It was sad. He was making himself sad, thinking about it. He'd missed all his chances. He'd made an unholy mess of things. And now it was too late to recover anything. There were no second chances, not ever . . .

Thinking about his life's work made him think about his life, of which he couldn't have too much left. Staring death in the face, he was. They all were. Impossible to brush it away now. The way of all flesh. They were all prey to it, death and the primeval angst: fear of same.

Or at least he was. And now for the first time he envied the Alzheimer's cases, so out of it that they didn't even know they were flesh, most of them, let alone realising that they were about to embark on the way of it . . . Not even knowing their own names, how should they be contemplating the imminent call of the Grim Reaper, the Great Leveller?

He smiled to himself. Did that make it more palatable, couching the matter in terms which conjured up memories – not of funeral parlours, muted sobbing, the sickly smell of wilting lilies and freshly turned sods – but of schoolrooms, of cold hard benches on the backs of knobbly young knees, of dog-eared poetry books clutched in sticky fingers, of a young life barely embarked on, instead of an old life winding down to its unremarkable end?

Too late now for disputations on the meaning of life. It had been too late even in the Centre; for him, anyway, although he'd indulged Annie who (unless he'd completely misunderstood her) had managed to find some meaning at last.

What had she said, exactly, that day on the hill, that last day when he'd been torn in two, so torn that he'd even considered the possibility later – when the die had been cast and he'd opted for Claude and the gang, and not by choice either, because who in their right minds would? – of trying to find her again. Annie in her cool white dress and gorgeous auburn hair, looking for all the world like a Botticelli angel, didn't she know?

Telling him that she'd found the way. And didn't HE know then and now, just what she had meant? That she'd embarked on the narrow way while he was bent on skidding right on past her along the other, the broad one, the one that led to destruction, in the company of Claude, Koksie, and Floors. Or Fatarse. What did it matter? There was nothing to choose between any of them. They all looked the same with their puffy purple faces, bloodshot eyes, straggly hair, blackened teeth and scabby necks.

Had he fallen prey to PRIDE for heaven's sake, at that already late, too late, stage of his miserable life? Was it pride that had made him spurn her offer of help? That. Or perversity.

Whatever the reason, he had chosen to go with Claude and the others straight into the maw of the abyss for a little foretaste of hell.

For the second time! And now here he was, still trying to escape his demons, the seducing spirits that never ceased tormenting him: Mave with her great heaving, sweating body, frothing on about her conjugal rights to which she had no right, strictly speaking, since they'd never actually made it to the altar.

And what about HIS rights? She'd really expected him to slaver over her pendulous old paps, hanging low and listless as sails in the doldrums – if that wasn't too much of a conceit. But he had seen bosoms in full sail, as it were. Not his mother's. Before she'd become shapeless as a ragdoll she'd been sleek and slim, with a little swell and surge, a ripple in the right light, that was all.

Corseted up, though, Mave had been like a man-o'-war, bosom like twin figureheads over the cutwater of her belly, imperious, bearing down on everyone like the old Queen Mary – the Queen Consort, not the ocean liner . . . Although come to think of it, that too . . .

He'd been terrified of her ever since she'd first squashed his unsuspecting face into those mounds ribbed with whalebone and unyielding as the hull of a galleon. And later that night, after the reception they'd had in lieu of a wedding, when she'd changed into her shortie pyjamas and feathery *peignoir*, she'd almost suffocated him, pressing his face into the cleavage between those now deboned and quivering outcrops. He'd thought his end had come. Done to death by dugs.

Annie, now. There had been a neat shape. Not overstated, but not understated either. She'd made just the right sort of statement. Not that she would ever have believed it.

But it was too late for all that now. His time had almost come. He was so near the end of his life that its meaning, for what it was worth, was a *fait accompli* and he was on his way to his reward, as they said; although that thought made him wonder if he had ever done anything to merit a reward.

He hadn't been the best of sons; not the worst, but not the best either. He'd learned how to take care of number one early on. His youth was pretty well misspent when it came to matters like rewards, for which he presumed one had to have done something GOOD. Did not having done anything all that bad either count as something good, he wondered? He had been no better, and no worse, than most people. But was that good enough?

The nuns would probably have insisted on a GOOD, a palpable, demonstrable, good. And the priest also. He'd have to get hold of the man, Rudy resolved, although he was a very difficult man to get hold of, judging from the way he hurried in and out, pretending not to hear his name being called, the cries of Father! Father Lacey! and Priest! that followed him around when he did visit. The only way to get hold of him was literally, to dig one's nails in and hang on until he sat down.

Not that Rudy blamed him. It was sheer purgatory, listening

to some of them, most of them, yammering on and on about who knew what; their relatives, known only to them, their parents, long dead.

But he'd have to do it, grab hold of him, and hopefully the priest would realise that he, Rudy, was different, that he had something to say, something sensible, and real questions to ask, about eternity, moral choices and value systems. And whether it would count in his favour that he was now living an absolutely exemplary life, even if he hadn't much choice to speak of any more?

That was the sort of question the priest should be able to answer, and convince him, Rudy, that it was still relevant, that the universe was not indifferent to them now, at the end of their quest, and about to be reaped and gathered in by Father Time.

And while he was about it he might even ask him what he thought of Freud, and Darwin, and maybe even Marx, Galileo and Newton, now that they'd been rehabilitated, or so he'd heard.

Seriously though, what of the bad things he might have to answer for, the undeniably bad things?

He had, after all, been in jail awaiting trial for Interference (he'd never been able to bring himself to qualify it, because it hadn't been sexual, not really, whatever the law had said, and Evadne). He hadn't interfered with Lillith. She'd interfered with him. But she'd been under age and he hadn't. He should have discouraged her; at the very least not have encouraged her, when he saw that the crush she had on him was taking a form best left unspoken, the lust (would that one could at least have called it love!) that could not speak its name, *verboten* fruit as it was.

He'd been sinned against, really, he'd been provoked and titillated. But that hadn't been the way the law had seen it. And that episode (together with the sentence, suspended it was true, even though Lillith had wept and wailed so much and so convincingly that he was expecting nothing less than the gallows), that episode had pushed him over the edge. The jail, Lillith's accusations, Evadne's contempt, the publicity, the ostracism, being destitute and homeless, had resulted in the breakdown that had put him in the psychiatric hospital for the first time, and caused the fatal weakness in his psyche, the weak link in his chain of control, rather like a badly set fracture that always snaps at the same place; the thin, frayed part of the rope, giving way at the slightest strain.

Although that had turned out to be fortuitous in a way because it had led to his meeting Annie in that other psychiatric institution, the second one. Be grateful for small mercies, as Sister Mary Ambrose was fond of saying.

But did all that suffering count? Would the guilt have been expiated by the time spent in jail, and the hospital, especially the time when there hadn't been an Annie, the first time which had been the worst? Had he redeemed himself in some measure? Would he still be called to account in eternity, if there turned out to be an eternity?

He couldn't wait for the priest who only came to say his incantations and sprinkle his holy water when someone was dying or had died. He, Rudy, needed to sound someone out on it immediately. But who? Not Laetitia. She'd only tell him it was 'hokaay', and not to 'warry', without grasping the complexity, not to mention the gravity, of it all.

Sister Mary Benedict then, not because he valued her opinion all that much, but because she just happened to be passing and slowly enough not to be on any particular errand. And then from the look of her, her tightly compressed lips and suspicious squint, she'd be bound to tell him the worst of it and he preferred that; it was too late for anything else . . .

Then again, if what she said confirmed his worst fears —

that he was too bad even for purgatory – he could always tell himself that she wasn't looking at him at all, but at old Neville McNaughton in the other corner of the room, or at the sides of her own nose.

'Sister,' he said. 'Do you think, if we have paid for our sins here on earth by various trials and tribulations, that we will be called on to pay again in the hereafter?'

To his surprise she looked as if that was exactly the question she was expecting someone, maybe even him, to ask, because she pounced at once:

'And what do you know about it?' she demanded. 'You're the guilty one then? Naughty old man, was it you? Sister Mary Bartholomew's told us all about you!'

Which could only have been a lie (or misapprehension, rather, seeing the woman was in orders and one should always have respect for the cloth) because he had no idea what 'it' could possibly be. But remonstration was useless. In Sister Mary Benedict's book he had incriminated himself beyond all recovery.

'You're needing a rap on the knuckles then, my man,' she pronounced menacingly, lips pursing to the point of bloodlessness. 'And see if I don't just give it you!'

Useless to ask what he was supposed to have done, what in fact must have been done by someone else. She didn't believe a word of it.

'We're going to have to lock the kitchen AND the pantry,' she threatened.

'Ah. Someone's been nicking food then?' he asked with an innocence so exaggerated that he sounded guilty.

'Don't you go pretending with me, my man!' she blustered. 'We'll be searching your room, see if we don't!'

He sagged with relief. 'You're welcome,' he said. 'You're more than welcome.'

And by then, of course, his sense of urgency concerning the moral issues or indeed issues of any sort (because there was still and had always been, that tug towards nihilism) had evaporated.

Reality intruded. He was amongst naughty old people who nicked things from the kitchen when the nurses' and Sisters' backs were turned. Evil had become trivialised in this final antechamber to eternity, and they had all become like naughty children. But wouldn't that, at least, count in their favour when the day of reckoning came? If it came? That they had become like little children?

Strange that anyone would bother to nick food when they were always complaining about it, and were almost disgusted with Rudy for eating everything on his plate – he who had always prided himself on his discerning palate – and it was true that some meals were unappetising, to say the least: the chicken *à la* king with the bits of green pepper that looked like something the sway-backed cat had sicked up, sausages that were squelchy in the middle, soya mince like polystyrene pellets, and all tasting exactly the same (how had they managed that, Rudy had often wondered; a feat, surely, to make beef stew taste like mealie meal porridge, which was what everything tasted like, come to think of it).

But then, he'd only to remember his days in the park and – on the rare occasions when such luxuries presented themselves – what his meals were like, for the current fare to approach gastronomical perfection, comparatively speaking.

Life had been dicey; to find oneself in the morning, still alive and more or less warm and dry, was a major victory. The others had adapted, most of them, but they had been 'homeless' longer than he had. In any case, he had never truly, in his heart of hearts, considered himself one of them. He was engaged in researching the plight of the drifter, he had told himself, and was play-acting to that end.

Or at least that was what he'd been able to tell himself the first time around, post-Evadne and post-jail when he'd been befriended by Muddy Waters, Pypsie Fraser and Nollie, who had had such a foul mouth that Rudy was convinced the poor man had Tourette's and should have received treatment rather than lose his job and end up in the park.

Rudy had been relatively young then so he'd managed for a time at least to affect a jaunty aplomb, a Chaplinesque demeanour (he had after all simply fallen on hard times, temporarily, like the little tramp). He'd tried to cultivate a resilience, to maintain an inner purity untouched by his sordid circumstances; and he had, he felt, carried it off well enough.

The others had respected him, considered him a gentleman, he felt sure. After all he hadn't looked at all like them, with their matted hair, puffy skin, bleary eyes, encrusted teeth and evil-smelling breath. He hadn't been down and out long enough.

He had tried to preserve the niceties, anyway. He'd dipped three fingers in the lily pond every morning to slick down his hair (resisting the temptation of goldfish-on-a-stick over a low fire for breakfast only because they were so scrappy, all fins and tails, the larger koi together with the ducks having long since disappeared), and another finger to wipe each eye. His teeth had to wait until the attendant had unlocked the public convenience – the water in the pond being too murky by far – for a quick swish or two at the basin, a scrub with a finger and a pick with a fingernail. Which was hardly enough of course, but more than the rest of them ever bothered to do. In any case, anything more than that was considered 'ablutions', and the attendant didn't allow people to perform ablutions in the public convenience.

After that it was out on the job of scrounging whatever could be scrounged, each of them heading for their designated intersections or corner cafés where they begged for loose change, since they hadn't eaten for three days, or four, depending on what they thought they could get away with.

Offering to work for food was a bit tricky, of course. They all valued their independence as entrepreneurs, albeit in the most informal of all of society's sectors.

Pretending to be war veterans wasn't a good idea. Most of them were too young to have served in the Second World War, and too old for Angola. He himself had never considered it, except on one occasion when he'd seen a number of old medals with their ribbons in the Pawn Shop; but the outlay was too great and the return too uncertain.

He wasn't a war veteran, anyway. He was Chaplin, the ageless *ingénu*, the innocent abroad. Life was a comedy: slapstick when the police tried to flush them out of the bushes and they scattered, running into trees, falling into ponds; poignant when they told their stories, Nollie and Pypsie and the rest of them, trying to make light of their personal tragedies. Laughter masked the pain of degradation; nothing was real, not the fights for discarded newspapers and cardboard boxes which when pressed flat could be sold by the kilogram (and how comical that had been, trying to flatten the resistant cardboard when they were so inebriated that they could barely stand) nor the pushing and shoving to get at cigarette butts which, all put together, sometimes made a passable smoke.

They were comedians, all of them, woebegone, to be sure, but with a whimsical response to most of life's vicissitudes, like the time when Pypsie Fraser had been pulled feet first from his stormwater pipe, insisting that he'd heard a baby cry far up the pipe, or perhaps it was only a kitten? They'd booked him for vagrancy and having no fixed abode. Pypsie had been indignant. 'My abode is fixed,' he'd declared. 'I'd like to see

59

you unfix it, unless you've got a jackhammer, or a bulldozer, or dynamite.' But stormwater pipes didn't count as an abode, they'd told him. 'But if I abode there it's my abode,' he'd insisted.

They'd all laughed at that. What else could they do? Comedy kept them going, kept them in command of situations that were always threatening to blow them away.

He'd played the game as well as any of them; he'd learned the tricks, used the cardboard placard, pleading: 'No job, 6 kids please help', or words to that effect; he'd hung around outside the take-away establishments looking hungry, outside bars looking thirsty and at bus stops looking tired.

One soon learned which cafés to frequent and which to avoid (word was passed about proprietors who called the police and laid false charges, or who had buckets of ice-cold water handy, especially in winter). He'd hung around outside the banks and ATMs too and he'd managed as well as the rest of them, he thought; even better sometimes, when people fancied they'd recognised someone of some worth who must genuinely have fallen on hard times, his accent and vocabulary having stood him in good stead.

And through it all he'd managed to preserve his self-respect by pretending to be engaged on important research, recording what his enquiring mind had gleaned in one of his black notebooks (the others safely stowed away in his leather suitcase which he'd booked in at the baggage office at the station), projecting an adventurous spirit, a devil-may-care master-of-his-fate stance while asking, quite casually:

'You wouldn't have cash for a pint, now would you? Daren't be out on a job like this carrying a wallet, you know. Be as much as my life's worth . . . All but dying of thirst just now . . .'

It had worked too, his pose of journalist on assignment, and it would work, as long as he did not become too much like them, like Muddy Waters who never washed and whose grimy skin with his bright, bloodshot blue eyes and tangled blond hair gave him a golliwog-in-negative look, or foul-mouthed Nollie, another one for the white-jacket brigade.

Compared with them he had been an amateur, an outsider, but tolerated, because who were they, the rejected, to reject anyone else?

And so he'd pretended to be one of them, easy enough most times, especially when he was a bit addled by the Klippies cocktail Muddy was famous for, his 'Red Lady', a mixture, Rudy had gathered, of brandy, strawberry jelly crystals, a dash of meths and water, although the resultant colour was nearer mud – the colour, in fact, of old Muddy himself – depending on how much water he added, and whether or not the water was clear. Lily-pond water, for instance, gave the mixture a strange olive cast, due no doubt to the presence of algae.

Still, he had survived (he'd been much younger, of course, that first time around), he had even thrived in his preferred persona of gentleman tramp, buffeted by life's storms, but unfailingly optimistic, smiling at adversities, responding bravely to injustices – like being chased and kicked from one end of the park to the other – right at the nub of things, but coolly detached, the quintessential spectator . . .

And what of THE injustice, the one that had put him out on the street in the first place? He didn't want to think about it but he was caught short; he had become incontinent, mentally, he'd lost control and his memories simply dribbled out all over the place: the court case, his breakdown, the shame and embarrassment of it all . . . Because the papers had got hold of the thing and there it was, large as life, plain for all to see: CITY MAN IN COURT FOR CHILD MOLESTATION. Name, address, photograph, everything. He'd never forgiven Evadne for giving them the photograph. Then again, Lillith may have been behind that little piece of mischief. She'd blown the whistle on him, hadn't she? But why? Had she just grown tired of the games in the library, such as they were? Because as he had sworn in court again and again, NOTHING HAD HAPPENED. On his life, his mother's life, the life of the Professor of Tonsorial Artistics, nothing had happened. Nothing to speak of, a little slap here, a little tickle there. That was all.

All right, then, a little slap on her pantied backside some-times, once or twice on her bare bot, a little tickle – nowhere too personal, nowhere too private, he swore. Most of it had taken place in his mind. So how could she have known?

She'd grown tired of him, that was it. The girl was a menace. Jailbait. She'd led him on and then shopped him. He'd taken no more than a nibble and she'd sprung the trap . . .

Because nothing had happened, nothing really; the court had established that much in the end and he got a warning, and a suspended sentence. Had she done it BECAUSE nothing had happened, he'd often wondered. Pique, then? Could the child really have considered herself a woman scorned? What on earth was the world coming to?

Or had she seen him as an interloper and resented his marriage to her mother? The possibilities – most of them Freudian – were truly endless and would have been fascinating to contemplate if it hadn't been his skin on the line.

Of course it was the end of Evadne and such relationship as they had had, which also wasn't much. He saw them all again, cringed at the expressions of outrage on their faces, the prosecutor, the judge and Evadne. And Lillith, her cheeks and eyes red and puffed from crying (what had she had to cry about?), sweet injured innocence, self-righteous indignation . . . They'd done him in, what was left of him after the arrest, indictment and incarceration.

Would he ever forget? That grey stone jail with other

awaiting trialers in their cages, with their hollow haunted eyes. No wonder he had been catatonic with shock, a condition which had ensured a lengthy postponement while he underwent psychiatric assessment, with the threat of aversion therapy – electric shocks, the other sexual offenders had explained, to his privates, while they showed him pictures of little girls.

So he'd stayed catatonic, that is, on his feet, with his mind blank and his face expressionless, while he'd been not exonerated exactly, but declared of sound mind and given the benefit of the doubt, since Lillith's story had changed so often that even Evadne had begun to look frustrated.

Not that that had helped. It was over. His life. He was out on the street. And then he'd broken down good and proper. It had all been too much for him. Clinical depression. Suicidal. Which was why he'd been committed for treatment, not once but twice, although the second time he'd met Annie and that had been some compensation.

At any rate, the mere threat of the aversion therapy had worked and he'd developed a healthy distaste for little girls, especially precocious, flirty little girls who played with the tops of their stockings . . . Which led him to wonder – his thoughts still dribbling on – now that they wore pantihose, what did they play with, the little nymphets, the shameless little chippies . . . ?

The hospital had been a treat, after all that (he'd had shock treatments, it was true, but mercifully they'd applied the electrodes to his temples and not somewhere else).

And then the second time around there had been Annie. She had believed in him. She had restored his sense of self-worth. She had taken him seriously. She had been genuine. She had been a tonic. And she had been too good for him. He'd always said that; not in those words exactly, but he'd respected her, paid homage in a way. She'd been too good for him; and

63

while he was ashamed to admit it, even to himself, she had also been too poor.

That had surprised him at first, because she had presented wealthy, like Evadne, and even Mavis. Evadne, well-feathered, wealth with class. Too old for him of course, but unfailingly generous until the Lillith débâcle. And Mave, also well on in years, although at that time he had been older as well. Mavis, Mave, not quite as wealthy as Evadne, but very comfortable. Comfort without class.

So what was he saying? That the woman who had it all didn't exist? Truism to end all truisms.

One had only to look at their end to gauge their beginnings and here in the Home he saw them at their inglorious end: shades of grey with spectacles, most of them; swollen knees, crooked toes, bent fingers, yellow fingernails, false teeth (PATENTLY false teeth, not the all-but-real kind one could get these days), hairnets pulled down low over their foreheads, shuffling around in their stained slack-suits and snagged jerseys.

He should have stuck with Annie. Annie had had real class, if not real money.

He heard her voice again, pleading with him: *Come with me. I can help you.*

He might have done too, if Claude and the others hadn't been on the Hill that day, with Koksie and Floors. He hadn't wanted to involve her with them. In any case, he'd made up his mind. He'd already said his piece, just as he'd planned to, although the Kipling quotation had been the inspiration of the moment. *A woman is only a woman, but a good cigar is a smoke . . .*

He hoped she had realised that he'd had to be ruthless so as not to be overwhelmed by tenderness. Then again, the devil of it was that, given his experiences with women, and the (admittedly) one experience of a Montecristo No. 5, he'd more than half meant it, he really had . . .

Looking back on it all now (not that he wanted to, but such was the malfunctioning of the mental equivalent of his sphincter), on the incredible botch he'd made of everything, he would have liked to see himself as a tragic figure, the anti-hero of a *comédie noire*.

But it hadn't really been like that. More like a comic strip actually, with him the eternal loser, an ageing Charlie Brown, Beetle Bailey or some such, with the events of his life nothing more than a weak joke, the sort of joke that made one groan with existential pain.

FIVE

LURCHING ALONG

They were all in the dining-room, jabbering away excitedly, decibels rising. Everyone talking and no one listening.

They were high, Rudy thought. High on the company, the tea, and the polony sandwiches. Gay, as if it were a party. Jaws snapping like grunters as they clamped worn-down false teeth on the crusts, tugging at them and trying to talk at the same time.

'. . . piles of newspapers in the bathroom. And rats. Breeding. I heard them. I heard their little feet pattering on the paper in the middle of the night . . .'

'. . . only way I could get away from that infernal gramophone . . .'

'Strong hands, but covered in operation scars . . .'

'. . . right there, plumb in the middle of my coconut ice!'

The conversations were as disjointed as they had been in the hospital, or at the Aftercare Centre, like little scraps of information coming through a faulty old Tannoy system.

Although that could have been because of his ears. Wax, Laetitia had said. Maybe he needed a teaspoonful of his mother's hot sweet oil to melt it all down again . . .?

Rudy got up to join Lyle Hargood and Neville McNaughton.

'Dry with it, though, except when a storm was brewing,' Lyle was saying, 'always grand and terrifying, the way the thunderwind would blow up suddenly, sweeping through the trees . . .'

He had a way with words, the old man. He'd had to have done something more than run a nursery, but when Rudy tried to draw him out he hadn't been forthcoming at all. He would talk about nothing but the Lowveld. Living almost entirely in the past had to be some sort of defence mechanism, Rudy decided, to counter the tedium of the present.

It was what he himself was doing, more and more. Parking in another time and place.

'Dry,' Neville McNaughton started up. 'AND hot. Sand in your eyes, under your tongue. Grit between your bloody teeth. Dust-devils and mirages. Had its moments, though. The sunsets . . .'

'Like a hothouse with all that moisture in the air,' Lyle murmured.

Neville ignored him. 'Colours you wouldn't believe. Greys and golds, mauve and blue in the distance.'

'Been to God's Window?' Rudy asked, remembering Evadne and their honeymoon trip to the Kruger Park and surrounds.

'How's that?' Neville asked, tapping on the floor with his walking stick.

'God's Window. Supposed to be like a view from heaven. Or into heaven, I don't remember which.'

'Ask Hargood then,' Neville snapped. 'He'll know.'

'Deep dark evergreen world, profuse with fungus and fern . . .'

'Is that a poem?' Rudy asked.

'Is what a poem?'

'What he's saying.'

'What's he saying? Who?'

'Lyle. Never mind.' Rudy sighed.

'Never MIND? Don't start something you're not planning to finish,' Neville said irritably.

Grumpy sort, Rudy decided. Apoplectic. Grogblossomed nose. Legacy of past indulgences, no doubt, since there was no opportunity for anything like that in the Home. Which may have been his problem.

One of the pickled bum faces leaned over and plucked urgently at his sleeve. 'When I go,' she said speaking through a mouthful of half-chewed bread and polony, 'I want the Salvation Army to have my things.'

'The old Sally Army! Been decent to me, too,' Rudy said. 'On a number of less than auspicious occasions.'

'C of E myself,' Neville snorted.

'What's that got to do with it?' she asked, peering venomously at him. 'Always been DRC MYself but it was the Salvation Army that did the most for us during the Depression.'

'And the evenings,' Lyle mused, 'alive with noise, frogs and crickets, squeaking bats and of course the nightjars . . .'

'Put a sock in it why don't you,' she told him contemptuously.

'Here! Why don't you put a bloody cork in it,' Neville said, banging with his stick. To Rudy's surprise she subsided at once, turning away from them.

Tea was over and the conversation, such as it was, came to an end. It would never be coherent or conclusive, Rudy realised. Whatever sense there was to be made of it would have to be made in one's own imagination, one's piecing together of the snippets like the pieces of a jigsaw puzzle. Or stay out of it altogether, simply letting it wash over one, like the noise of the crickets and frogs in the night.

Only that would leave him with nothing but his own past, and he didn't much want to live there, any more than in his present.

As for the future, there wasn't one to speak of. They all knew that. Maybe the difference was that they knew it better than he did. Maybe the terrible truth hadn't filtered down to really take hold of his consciousness. And when it did, he feared – or should he be relieved? – he'd become just like them, endlessly mulling over the past, or those parts which could be remembered, like what had happened during the Depression, or in Bahrain; what the Lowveld had been like, the fact that rats used to breed in the bathroom, and even what Alistair, or Douggie or whoever, had been doing behind the tree in the park.

They all had their memories. Unlike Lyle's, though, or even Neville's, his didn't bear recounting. His were either too sordid or too sad.

After the untimely demise of the Professor of Tonsorial Artistics, for instance, he and his mother discovered that far from being the owners of a 'little goldmine', the Salon, they were bankrupt, the Professor having operated on a vast over-draft, with such cash flow and liquidity as there had been having long since been lost on a succession of no-hope horses.

They had had to remove from their comfortable semi-detached in Central (it having been attached by the clerk of the court, together with everything in it) to a residential hotel in South End, which sounded grand enough but was in reality a glorified doss-house where they were accommodated in one of two backyard rooms, the 'Annexe', so-called, but which was in fact no more than an outbuilding, originally intended for servants.

Both rooms looked out on an unevenly paved concrete courtyard from a narrow stoep enclosed by a rotting wooden railing, and straight into the uncurtained window of an antiquated bathroom with a rusty iron bath standing on broken gryphon claws next to a blackened toilet with overhead cistern and chain.

The place was almost, but not quite, an historical monument with the delivery of water and electricity both fitful and hazardous. It seriously depressed his mother who spent most of the time prostrate and weeping in her corner of the gloomy room they shared, her face becoming even more puffy and amorphous in the process, and when it got too much for him Rudy would go out and sit on the step outside where the establishment's black cat would nudge, paw and butt him, hoping for attention, or food.

When the worst of her grief had spent itself his mother had unpacked – with due ceremony – the Professor of Tonsorial Artistics' dress shirt with the onyx studs and cuff-links to match.

The Professor, she informed him, had last worn them to the Hairdressers' Union Annual Award Dinner-Dance where he had been presented with the framed accolade which had always hung in the Salon and which had unfortunately been attached by the clerk of the court, together with everything else, perm machines, hair-driers, furniture and fittings, lotions and pomades, before she could take it down and hide it.

She also informed him that she intended to apprentice him, Rudy, as soon as he was old enough and that he would one day wear the same dress shirt to the Annual Award Dinner-Dance, or at least the studs, or at the very least (because who knew how fashion might change in the interim?) the cuff-links.

In the mean time she solemnly charged him to find the accolade which must have been sold in a job lot by the auctioneer. It was, she said, part of his inheritance and would one day be his inspiration.

But Rudy had spent enough time in the Salon to know that Tonsorial Artistics was not for him. Not for him the spending of endless hours sweeping hair up off the dusty floors as an apprentice, or worse still, having to touch it, especially when wet . . . He'd as soon become a dentist and poke around in people's rotting teeth.

He'd had his own ideas, even then, but there were still so many of them that he hadn't been able to make a definite choice, so he had merely smiled his sweet acquiescent smile which made his overbite seem less prominent, shelving the matter of a career until it simply had to be addressed.

In the event, his mother had also passed on just after he'd completed his matric (at great sacrifice to her and with the help of some of her clients of long standing who had tracked her down to the Main Street Salon where she'd begun working as an assistant) and before he'd had to make a final decision on the direction his future would take.

What ambitions had he had, though? He hadn't distinguished himself academically. Throughout his school career he had been labelled a 'dreamer' though what he'd spent his schooldays dreaming about he could not now remember.

He'd had only vague interests in a number of directions, the most compelling (if that was not too strong a term) being literary. He had loved books and had read everything he could lay his hands on, developing in the process a very catholic taste.

It may have been because of that vagueness, that lack of real commitment to anything in particular, and the refusal of his mother's clients to contribute another penny to his education – he having failed, as was said, to distinguish himself in any way apart from essay writing and there not being many career prospects in that line – that had caused him to more or less fall into his first job as a cub reporter at the local newspaper, a job he'd hated and from which escape was his only option.

Escape had always been Rudy's reaction to pressure, boredom, dissatisfaction and unhappiness. He'd always been able to find a bolt-hole, even as a young lad, when the bioscope had been his substitute for reality and his refuge from the stress of school and the loneliness of home. The bioscope had given him access to a world of glamour and intrigue, beautiful women and handsome resourceful men, of love and sacrifice, hate and revenge, courage and passion.

He had been drawn into it body and soul. He'd lost himself in the cool dark interiors, luxuriating in the plush seats, the moulded, frescoed walls, the ornate proscenium arches festooned with plaster cupids, grapes, drapes and garlands. He'd wondered at the intricately pleated sateen curtains which could be drawn up into myriads of tiny folds, loops and shiny swags, or across the stage with heavy swirls by the audibly clanking backstage machinery.

And so, when his job had begun to exasperate him beyond endurance Rudy had simply ducked into the nearest cinema, telling himself that whatever the news editor had had in mind for him to do along the lines of neighbourhood notes and crime watches, he was preparing himself to apply for something much more congenial: the position of movie critic.

Of course by then much of the magic had gone. He knew what lay behind the screen now: grimy reality, dusty ropes and pulleys, fused lights, stove-in trunks, broken seats and empty boxes . . . The stuff of life itself.

The films weren't the same any more either. There'd been no replacements for Gish and Garbo, Helm and Harlow, Ward and West. The comedies weren't quite so funny any more; the melodrama never quite as affecting. He'd been able to laugh until he cried at Buster Keaton in shrunken suit and stoneface, at Ben Turpin, all cross-eyes and walrus moustache, and Fatty Arbuckle looking permanently surprised. He'd been devoted to Bara and Bow, Fairbanks and Chaney, Rathbone and Lugosi. He'd liked the predictability of the films. Nothing there of the terrifying haphazardness of real life, its mundaneness, its meanness . . .

What he had seen since those days hadn't impressed him too much. It had become too gory by half, too *outré*. Realism gone rank, smelling to high heaven. Bodily functions hung out like laundry for all to see . . . The mystery, the magic had gone; morality as well. No subtlety, just in-your-face rub-your-nose-in-it sort of stuff, the hero as bad as the villain and nothing to choose between them any more. No one believed in anything, hoped for anything; it was just a question of staying alive at any cost as far as he could see.

Imagine any of the new breed of hero getting down on his knees to repent like Clark Gable had done at the end of 'San Francisco', while MacDonald warbled *Nearer my God to Thee* and the violins sobbed in the background.

Corny, even then, but it gave one a good feeling. It gave some point to the whole exercise of life.

So, what was the world coming to?

Of course his world then had come to an abrupt end when he wasn't able to produce the required copy on local events or the crimes he'd been meant to cover. He had produced some neat little essays of a philosophical nature on the criminal mind and the importance of leisure activities and recreation, but no FACTS, and FACTS, the news editor had informed him, were what newspapers were all about. With his severance pay in his pocket and feeling very hardly done by, Rudy had taken himself off to the bioscope.

How he missed it now. If only he'd been able to get to the bioscope occasionally, he wouldn't have minded the lack of congenial company in the Home so much.

Although, as he reminded himself, bioscopes weren't quite the same any more. They were called cinemas now, little claustrophobic places that sucked one right into the middle of the oversized screen making the aggression and gore even more of an in-your-face experience. There was no backing away, even in the last row, because they were right there, the new breed of leading man and woman, without style or stature, without clothes for much of the time, bleeding, vomiting, urinating, copulating, right between your eyes, doing things not even old Floors would do in public.

Nor did that other substitute, television, satisfy him. It was a different sort of thing. It wasn't a whole new world, dark and exciting. It was an appliance, like a toaster.

So now at the end, there was nothing for it but to sit out the rest of his life in the fraying wicker chair, looking out to sea, the writing pad on his lap, pen in one hand, spectacles in the other (they had soon realised that he was barely able to see close up and had provided him with funny little half-moon reading glasses).

Still, it wasn't too bad a life, the querulousness of his companions notwithstanding. It could have been worse. No one whacked, prodded or even nudged him with a nightstick or baton or whatever they were called these days. Some of the black nurses could be shrill, some of the nuns short-tempered, but there was no one too terrifying and nothing too threatening in the Home.

He could reminisce, fantasise, call up the old images, remember the glamorous old movie queens in their two-tone pointy-toed shoes and cloche hats, pulled down low over one dark kohl-rimmed eye.

It might have been that that had drawn him to Annie in the first place. The way she'd worn her yellow beret pulled down over one dark-rimmed eye. Although those deep shadows had been due to nervous exhaustion and not kohl. Or the result of the electroconvulsive therapy perhaps; depression certainly, and drugs, probably. But whatever the cause the look had been the same, wounded and vulnerable. World-weary and slightly worn . . .

Like the divine Dietrich who wore her own nose and teeth, not perfect by today's plastic standards, but REAL, a beauty she'd been born with.

Those were the days, of course, when even the male stars were slim, fragile, almost feminine in their beauty. Navarro, Valentino, Gilbert, Barrymore . . . sensitive, intelligent. No mindless muscle there. Long lean faces, aquiline noses, high foreheads and smooth dark hair combed straight back, or perhaps parted in the middle.

A little too much grease, perhaps, as the Professor of Tonsorial Artistics had speculated (pot calling the kettle black) while he was honing his cutthroat on the strop which hung next to the bathroom mirror, an activity which always made him more communicative.

Rudy was surprised at the little surge of nostalgia he felt, remembering the Professor and their conversations in the bathroom. Perhaps he should ask to be buried, or cremated, in the onyx studs and cuff-links? As a belated gesture of respect?

Looking back on his life and that of his mother and the Professor of Tonsorial Artistics', Rudy had come to realise more and more that he was like them, one of the little people (the little grey people, even) who made no impression on the world, left no mark, had nothing to show for themselves, who were born, lived and died, leaving nothing behind but a few handfuls of ash or a casket of bones, depending on the method of final disposal.

The thought was intolerable to him. If that were really the way of it, it made life meaningless for all but the few achievers, the so-called movers and shakers who'd had an impact on history, or those who had managed to create something of more than ephemeral interest.

Was he one of those? He still had, ridiculously, the desire to write, to develop those few scraps and pieces he had carried in his notebooks through all the years.

Who to share them with, though? One had to be careful about that sort of thing, about whom one bared one's soul to.

He remembered once, his brain fuddled with the mixture Zolah had been ladling out all afternoon, scrabbling for the notebooks in the bottom of his suitcase, lately retrieved from the baggage counter at the station and now carefully hidden behind a clump of reeds on the far side of the duckpond.

Perhaps he'd needed reassurance at that time, when his life had reached its absolute nadir, dependent as he was then on the Sally Army and his pals in the park; perhaps he'd needed to remind himself of what he had once been, or had hoped to be.

Claude, ou Floors and Koksie Harmse had gone off to a shebeen with the money Zolah had earned in the damp sand under the promenade the previous night, so he had sat her down and begun to read.

Not the most discerning of audiences, of course, and he should have known better. In fact, he had barely begun when she said she'd got to 'go' and needed paper and tried to grab the notes.

It had been a tense moment for both of them, he remembered. But she may have been right. Maybe that was all they were good for.

Then again, they might be worth preserving after all. His *oeuvre*. Perhaps he should bequeath the lot to Annie. They always managed to trace people if an inheritance was involved.

Rudy smiled. Poor Annie, inheriting his nicked leather suitcase, his notebooks, the foxed poems, the Debenham portrait, the Professor's framed accolade and, if he didn't get buried or cremated in them, the studs and cuff-links. What would she make of all that?

Strange, the impulse to leave something of oneself behind, as if the leaving of a deposit of some kind gave meaning to life. But if it did then the meaning would surely be valid only if the deposit amounted to something? For the bulk of mankind, then, life was surely meaningless.

So then, what was the purpose of living? And living such complicated, complex lives, moreover, lives so fraught with joy, pain, fear, hope and love? Why, the very meanest lives, those lived by the homeless in park and bush on the very lowest levels of society, were lived with purpose as though they mattered; as though the very struggle to survive was somehow meaningful in itself, and made life worth while.

But in what way? If one pared life right down to the bone, so to speak, scraped away all the philosophies, religions, scientific and artistic achievements, histories, all the intellectual encrustations and extrusions, all the activities with which man sought to give meaning to his life, what was one left with? Man. A creature of intrinsic worth because he alone, of all creation, had a conscious sense of himself and his place in space and time. A sense that went well beyond instinct. Man in all his naked glory or shame, depending on one's viewpoint, for it was he who gave meaning to the said encrustations and extrusions after all. He himself. Just as he was. Naked in and naked out, to paraphrase Job.

Why so complex then? Was the earth really a battleground between opposing forces of good and evil with mankind the prize in the game? With one's decision for one or the other side governing one's eternal destiny? A conscious, considered decision on which path one wanted to take, such as Annie had been getting at, and the evangelicals insisted on?

If there were two opposing forces, independent of, and influencing man, depending on his free-will choice, it would seem that the majority had made the wrong choice, since on the face of it evil would appear to have had the upper hand throughout man's sorry history. Orthodoxy had always held that the creation had been good and evil had arisen as the result of man's wrong choice, his decision to rebel rather than obey.

And there was surely a case to be made that man had such a choice, or choices, throughout his life . . . As long as he had a serviceable conscience.

But there would have to be a reason for choosing either; a good reason for choosing good, in short, since if all men were like him, Rudy thought ruefully, the choice of evil over good was almost an automatic one, easier, and promising delights which admittedly never really materialised.

Which begged the question of what happened after death? Was there a judgement and eternal reward or damnation? What other incentive could there be for choosing the good and abstaining from the evil? Which in turn predicated a Judge who necessarily transcended both good and evil.

There was no getting away from it, certainly not at HIS time of life, not without closing one's eyes, ears and mind and playing the congenital idiot. And who knew what THEY knew about such matters; who knew but that they, having no minds to speak of, penetrated the mysteries effortlessly so that for them there were no questions of good or evil, no choices. Who knew? Certainly they could not be held accountable for their choices, if any. And there one was faced with a further presupposition. One that was unnerving, compelling, but in a way, strangely comforting: that of a Judge Who was not only transcendent, but just.

And now here he was at the end of it all. In his dotage, balding, rheumy and palsied, one of the wrinklies, blotchy, liver-spots on his hands, with stiffening joints and quivering jaws, but still on the hoof – if only just – still lurching along . . .

He'd shrunk, like a shoddy pair of long johns, as old Gladstone used to say. Although what on earth had suddenly brought HIM to mind Rudy didn't know. It seemed that his memories had taken to simply bubbling up like viscous matter through the deepening, widening faults and fissures of his sulci irrespective of the normal thought processes.

Fear old age, Plato had said, *for it does not come alone*. No. It came with disease and death. He knew it; they all knew it. No one mentioned it of course. It wasn't the sort of thing that was discussed in the Home, where death had become the obscene, the unmentionable, the unthinkable. Because they were all going to live for ever.

Of course, Rudy reflected, the awareness, the recognition of death, pervaded life almost from the beginning, or at least from the age of reason (Ma, why did Grandpa die? Will I die?). It was death, the fear of death, accepted in other times, but suppressed in our own, that contributed to the pervasive angst of our post-modern, not to mention post-Christian age. That was it, of course. Darwin, Freud, Marx, and the church's own fifth column, the higher critics, the demythologisers, had for ever smudged the neatly drawn Judaeo-Christian blueprint for life; had in fact, all but obliterated it, together with the old moral absolutes. *In those days there was no king . . .; everyone did what was right in his own eyes*. Which in practice meant nothing that gave meaning to life and therefore to death.

Wasn't that it? The *cri de coeur* of young and old: nothing to live for, nothing to die for, and nothing but opiates to ease the pain; not of life, or death, even, but the perceived irrelevance, the absurdity, of both.

The alternative was to go back then, to posit once again the idea of a plan and purpose for the universe, for man; the linear view of history, an ordained beginning and a predestined end. One had to recognise the duality, of good and evil, and the concomitants: righteousness and reward, sin and retribution, heaven and hell, the two paths, in short, the narrow and the broad . . . One had to have a king – or King – for history to make sense, for one to be able to live life and face death with some equanimity, if not confidence.

He'd better get hold of Father Lacey, then, shouldn't he? Make confession, receive absolution, make peace, come to terms with himself, in preparation for the journey ahead. That was simple enough, surely?

But would it count if one didn't really mean it, believe in it? If one were not motivated by true repentance but expediency, or fear . . .?

What to do then? Nothing, he supposed. As usual. Sweep death under the carpet where the rest of the detritus of his life already lay.

There was no point in asking any more questions. He'd spent his life asking all sorts of people all sorts of questions and he'd come no closer to finding the meaning of life, or death. He'd even tried to draw the Chief Psychiatrist out on the subject.

He remembered the day, or perhaps it should be A day, since there had been nothing really unique about it; in fact the only memorable thing was that, of all the memories of all the days his subconscious mind could have dredged up just then, it had chosen this one, presenting it to his consciousness as clearly as if he were reliving it. (Wasn't that a sign that he was near the end? Didn't they say that one saw one's life scrolling down before one? Or was that only if one were drowning?)

Anyway, he remembered it clearly. Cold and windy outside. Black south easter howling like a lost soul. New orange sun-filters giving the whole consulting room a warm glow as if a fire were burning there. He – the Chief Psychiatrist from Swakopmund – was as warm and cheerful, dapper in his dove-grey suit and shiny jackboots, fingering the little grey skull he used as a paperweight, opening it to reveal the grey plastic brain inside, closing it again with a snap. His attitude exuded *bonhomie*, soliciting confidences, practically IMPELLING one to talk.

But what to say? His thoughts had somehow fused, locked, shunted into one another and then derailed, in a sort of cerebral train smash.

He'd started muttering (one had to do something, the man expected it): 'OK. Perhaps I've never known, perhaps I've forgotten, or at least not consciously thought about it, not enough to give the thought a chance to take effect, to actually RESOLVE anything. I'm in something of a stew.'

'A suspended sentence isn't a stew,' the Chief Psychiatrist had chided. 'Being penniless, homeless, that's something else, but right now you're psychotic, my friend. Ample evidence of that. If it will give you some comfort . . . I mean, what have we got here? *"Anxiety . . ."* ' He began reading from Rudy's file: ' . . . *marked consciousness restriction, some loss of acuity of perception, over-activity of the central and autonomic nervous systems, palpitations, tremors, unpleasant epigastric sensations, tingling in the extremities, muscular tension, dizziness . . .'*

It was true. He'd been completely stressed out, waiting for the trial, the verdict; eaten up with animosity towards everyone and a deep suspicion that he had been snared in a web of malevolence, that he was being pushed to self-destruct, by them, the seducing spirits, the succubi . . . Evadne and Lillith.

The Chief Psychiatrist had leaned back, smiling, his lips very pink in the orange light. Had he really expected that litany of distress to comfort, reassure him, Rudy wondered.

'Well, my nerves were pretty raw,' he had agreed. 'Wanted to scream. Couldn't bear to be touched. My skin felt alive all over. Everything was out of focus. I was terrified.' It had been

81

his turn to lean back, amazed that he'd been able to articulate like that, to verbalise the thing, the pain that was beyond words, beyond description.

'Your parents, siblings, they haven't been supportive?'

He'd shaken his head. No parents. No siblings.

'Good thing, sometimes. Families tend to feed on each other's neuroses.'

Feed, he'd thought. Like leeches, limpets, suctorial annelids . . . 'They'd have been supportive if I'd had any,' he'd said. 'Sure they would.'

'Psychotic,' the Chief Psychiatrist continued amiably, stroking the little grey plastic brain. 'So dissociated that we couldn't talk.'

It all became too much for him then. 'Life isn't supportive, I mean, supportable,' he began to whine. 'I mean, I am without support . . .' Because it had dawned on him again, his future and what it didn't hold, perhaps could never hold, now that he had lost everything, had a police record and was broken in mind and spirit. 'It's easier to hurl in, to die . . .'

'Ah, to die,' the Chief Psychiatrist repeated with some satisfaction. 'I was waiting for you to come to that. As it says here — we've picked up on it, you see, know you better than your own mother — *"sense of unworthiness"* ', he began to read again, *'often morbidly exaggerated, rooted in fears and misgivings about moral worth, etc. Exaggerated feelings of failure, of having failed others, hence self-reproach, delusions of wickedness, unpardonable and deserving of punishment* . . . All very natural, in the circumstances.'

'That explains it then,' he'd said miserably. 'You've picked up on it all right. More than I've picked up on myself and that's saying something.'

The sarcasm was lost on the Chief Psychiatrist. 'What you must bear in mind,' he'd said very seriously, 'is that death is not even reported experience. Not even hearsay. It never becomes part of life's repertoire. After death, you see,' he smiled his pink smile, 'you don't have a repertoire. Which leaves us with your real problem. Life.'

'Life,' he'd echoed uncertainly. 'Isn't life, living, the prerogative of the sane?'

'Now don't go making categories like that,' the Chief Psychiatrist had said disapprovingly. 'They're too arbitrary. We'll smooth the edges for you, smudge the details. We've got the complete chemical arsenal; and the side-effects, a little dizziness, a black-out or two, loss of memory, some permanent blank patches perhaps, but better, you'll agree, than having every little nerve-racking thought make it across the synapses?'

He hadn't wanted to appear ungrateful. 'I'm not complaining,' he'd said. 'I don't mind that, the dizziness and all that. It's not the details, and the edges exactly. It's the sense of unreality. It's the way my thoughts just flit around. I can't catch them and assemble them and make sense of them. I don't mind the black-outs. It's like anaesthetic, that feeling of floating off into darkness. I love that. It's like dying . . . What I imagine . . .'

'My dear RK! Dying is something you need to consider only if you have to explain living. Now. How many ECTs have you had?'

He must have expressed resistance of some sort because the Chief Psychiatrist stared at him, pink lips pursed in mild disapproval. 'You don't care for them?'

'It's not THEM so much,' he'd explained, 'and I love the anaesthetic. It's the whole set-up that's so horrible, those cold little cubicles and the dusty curtains and that German nurse coming in with the blanket and hotwater bottle and asking, "Haf you got goot weins?" Every time.'

'We'll have a word with her,' the Chief Psychiatrist promised.

'And it's not only that,' he'd gone on (might as well have the whole thing out). 'It's that everyone looks so awful when they're wheeled out, with that dummy thing holding their tongues out and their faces all red and inflated, like a bicycle tube. And I know I'm going to look like that too, my face is going to be red and swollen, with that rubber thing on my tongue and saying "aaaaagh!" And all the time that music, that awful bland piped music: *Danau so blau* . . .'

'You shouldn't have been peeping,' the Chief Psychiatrist said. 'That's what the curtains are for. And what do you think we should be playing?'

But it had got beyond a joke by then. How should he know? Was there music to be convulsed by?

He'd shown him his forearms. 'Look,' he'd said. 'I'm stubbing my stogie out on them.'

'Good,' the Chief Psychiatrist said. 'I'm glad you brought that up. This might help you to understand.' He closed the little skull with a snap, opened the glass-fronted bookcase behind his desk and took out a novel by Grass. 'Here,' he said, leafing through it briefly and beginning to read: "*. . . one man held the patient's left arm, his dentist explains to Starnusch about dental methods of one hundred years ago, the second wedged his knee into the pit of his stomach, the third held the poor devil's right hand over a candle flame so as to divide the pain.*" That's what you've been doing. Dividing the pain.'

He'd looked pleased, as though he'd resolved the issue. But what about the real issue? 'What about the pain then?' Rudy had asked. 'There all the time, even when I've forgotten. The cause, I mean, the effect. The pain, it's still there, like a heavy weight, or a painful bruise . . .'

'All in good time,' the Chief Psychiatrist had promised. 'The medication will help, but you must learn how to react to all the pains and griefs natural to living, not to let them oppress and unsettle you, overwhelm you.'

'And if I can't? That's when oblivion is preferable, to become numb to everything, everyone, to die . . .' (And of course, it had been easy to talk that way about death then, in his early thirties; to be so cavalier about it.)

'Dying,' the Chief Psychiatrist had said firmly, 'is the one experience you'll be missing out on, strictly speaking. Because death doesn't exist, consciously, except in the minds of those who are left behind.'

'And after? Beyond death? Doesn't that bear worrying about?'

The Chief Psychiatrist had shrugged. 'Realm of philosophy. Outside my field. But seriously. You are coming out of it, you know. Slowly but surely. In fact, I'm going to give you a patch of earth.'

'A patch of earth?'

'And some spring bulbs. We've got a little garden going at the back of the hospital. Plant them and watch them grow. There's virtue in that, you know. Watching things grow. Very therapeutic.'

He was opening the door. The consultation was at an end, but Rudy hadn't been able to let it go at that.

'That impulse to commit suicide. I don't really want to die,' he'd admitted. 'But what else, considering the desperation and embarrassment . . .'

The Chief Psychiatrist had tugged at his lips, paler now in the greyish light from the long corridor. 'Suicide,' he'd said vaguely. 'Take my advice. Give the bulbs a try. Then we'll see . . .'

What a man, Rudy thought, the chief psychomancer from Swakopmund! Using the little skull and brain like worry beads. Now there was a psychoanalytic seam worth quarrying!

Since then he'd more or less come to terms with it. Life and death. *Memento mori.* In the midst of life we are in death. That sort of thing. Death an omnipresent dark shadow on the periphery of life. We'd all have to shuffle off the mortal coil sooner or later; which made it sound merely transitional, like a moth extricating itself from its pupa. Nothing too unnatural there. Evolutionary in a way. Another plane of existence. From one form to the next. Or to nothing. He hadn't quite made up his mind yet.

Nothing would be preferable in a way, he'd come to think. Because if there were something, one would have to prepare oneself for it somehow. But how, if one didn't know for sure what it was? How prepare for the unknown?

There was always the orthodox theological standpoint, of course, the Catholic credo. But purgatory wasn't too much comfort, not after one had lurched through life the way he had.

SIX

OPENING UP

The low moan, like a dozen distant lawnmowers, intruded on his reverie. It came from what Laetitia had called the 'frail frail-care', the assisted-living block, the smelly section, where the senile demented and the Alzheimer's cases were kept.

At least they were all still on the hoof, and even those who weren't, who were in wheelchairs by reason of amputations, embolisms, fractures and the like, could manage, more or less. He was able to do for himself as well, Rudy reflected, and he intended to go on for as long as he could since the smell of stale urine made him gag.

Old Lyle Hargood was still capable of lyrical flights and Neville McNaughton was reasonably spry, although he had become fixated on the war and its aftermath, always going on about what had happened 'up North'.

One did grow a bit tired of it. It was as though the man's life had stopped in 1945. Something must have happened. Shell-shock, nerve gas, the Bahrain sun?

'Gave him a bicycle,' he was saying. 'Not an education. Not a job. A bicycle. Told him to apply to the Post Office. That was the government for you. Made beggars of us all. Poor whites.'

'What would you say if I told you I was on the road myself once?' Rudy said on impulse. There. It was out. And what for? Just to jack up the conversation which was boring him to death? Killing him before his time? Or a reflex reaction to the group therapy session atmosphere? (Although group therapy, even with the rabid psychotics, had been a doddle compared with trying to make sense of this lot.) 'Well, not the road exactly, but that I had taken up residence, temporarily of course, and purely to do some first-hand research for a screenplay I was contemplating, in the park, rigged up a passable shelter behind the cannas, canopy of reeds, nicely lined with cardboard and newspaper, black refuse bags which are tolerably waterproof . . .'

'Cannas . . .' Lyle said thoughtfully, 'I can tell you . . .'

'HE did it in the park,' Edna Simpson-or-Something (Rudy hadn't been able to catch her surname) broke in. 'Alistair. Behind a tree. Thought no one was looking.'

'And just what WAS he doing, woman?' Neville asked. 'Because I presume YOU were looking?'

'Great clumps of colour,' Lyle said, 'primary and the hybrids, all along the roadside, growing from a few discarded bulbs . . .'

'Some things you WANT to see,' Edna said cryptically. 'And some things you don't.'

'Well then?' Neville insisted. 'Get on with it.'

But Edna had clamped her lips so tight she looked as if she would never open them again. Beyond the pale, Rudy decided, even apart from the fact that she had a dewlap like an old milch cow. Not that there was much to choose between any of them from that point of view. They all sagged all over the place, with pendulous pouches hanging from their upper arms, stomachs right down to their knees . . . Lumps and bumps filled with lard, skin all pitted and pocked like waterlogged oranges.

'The cannas,' Lyle said. 'Put me in mind of it just now. Could have lit out myself, once . . .'

'You mean, split?' Rudy asked, intrigued.

'What?' Neville looked suspiciously at him.

'Lighting out. Splitting.'

'You daft or what?'

'Because that's where he was standing, near the cannas, that snaky smartalecky fellow . . .'

'WHO?' Neville all but yelled, banging with his stick. 'What did you just say? What are you talking about? Snaky fellow? What snaky fellow?'

'Let him finish, why don't you?' Rudy said.

Neville continued to thump the floor with his walking stick as if words had failed him. But Lyle wouldn't say anything more.

Rudy heaved himself up. He'd just seen the physiotherapist go down the passage. She wasn't carrying her recorder and tapes so he knew she'd come from the frail-care section. He also knew she stopped for a cup of tea before she went home, always made for her personally by Sister Mary Bartholomew and brought on a tray with a biscuit or two. She was usually quite amenable to some conversation while she munched (while they both munched, since she'd always been willing to share her biscuits with him) although she didn't ever say much herself. A quiet girl, he'd found, and not all that unattractive either, although her hair was on the greasy side, and a bit wispy.

In any case, he'd made a point of cultivating her, joining her whenever he happened to see her, and now, having begun like the others to feel the need to unburden himself, to make disclosures, confessions of a sort, to open up in order to connect, to give someone something to remember him by, he'd brought along some folded pages he'd taken out of one of his black notebooks.

'A fragment, my dear,' he said, presenting them to her and lowering his neat white head and scrawny shoulders in a courtly bow, 'written in the days when de Gaulle was trumpeting through Europe like a rogue elephant . . .'

'De Gaulle?' She had a pronounced Afrikaans accent. Not unattractive. French was sexier, but what could one do?

'You have heard of de Gaulle?' he asked anxiously.

She smiled, her eyes brightening. It was true, then, he thought. No flies on her, as Lyle had said. Or had it been Neville?

'I didn't only do physio,' she said. 'I started with Political Science and History, but then, what do you do with it?'

'What indeed,' Rudy agreed. 'When in doubt, be pragmatic.'

She turned the title page on which he'd written only the de Gaulle quotation, unattributed (who on earth could remember who said what, considering all the things that have been said, he'd justified the omission at the time) before exclaiming: 'But that's MY name. Over and over. What do you mean? That about de Gaulle and then my name, over and over?'

'Your name?' He'd forgotten that he'd spent one entire afternoon writing Annie's name in the nearest he could get to a copperplate with the ballpoint pen he had nicked from Sister's office in the Aftercare Centre. 'Your name?' he asked again, sounding as querulous as she had. And tremulous too, he thought. His voicebox wasn't what it used to be, or maybe the tremor was caused by the sudden memory of that afternoon, when he'd put everything he had, everything he couldn't allow himself to think or feel – just then, anyway – into the writing, over and over again, of Annie's name.

'Why my name?' she insisted, becoming suspicious. 'I mean, what's it got to do with de Gaulle . . . trumpeting around?'

'That,' he said, 'was written AFTER de Gaulle had gone trumpeting around. Long after. But THAT name has always rung in my heart. Or nearly always. Anna . . . Anna . . . You know, like Roxanne . . .'

'Roxanne?'

She was quite a shrill little thing, he decided. Perhaps it had been a mistake, cultivating her. 'Your name, is it?' he asked blandly. 'How fortuitous. Quite my favourite name, my dear.'

'It's Annamarie, actually,' she said. 'But everyone always says Anna.' She pronounced it the Afrikaans way: 'Ahna'.

'That's all right then. It's my alltime greatest favourite name. Your name, actually? More than coincidence, my dear. Prescience, premonition, call it what you will . . .'

She wrinkled her eyebrows at him. Strangely they weren't quite complete. Missing in spots, a bit tufty, like her hair.

Suddenly he felt tired. Somehow the old spark had gone. Still, he wasn't about to give up just yet. Because what was he, if not adaptable, mentally flexible, a man of catholic taste and interests, the essential savant? And then, beggars couldn't be choosers, as he knew well enough from painful experience.

'Political Science, you say?'

'I don't know,' she said carelessly, wiping her fingers on a tissue and pushing the tray away. 'I don't remember much, actually. I only did it for a year. And I never understood much of it either.'

'All to do with power, my dear. The ones with the power and the ones without the power and wanting the power, and even the ones without the power and not wanting the power but not wanting anyone else to have it either . . . That's what they say. That's politics for you. And politicians. All possessed of the same low cunning. Janus faces, all of them. Which is what gave rise to this little piece, originally . . .' He tapped the pages which she'd left lying on the table.

'You're writing about politics?' She was gathering up her coat, trying to locate her car keys in the huge knapsack-like handbag she carried. 'But what for?'

'You mean, at this juncture? Well of course, you're right. We've gone a good way beyond "pieces". Need a bit more than that now, politically speaking.'

She stood looking at him, fingering her keys. 'I didn't know you wrote,' she said at last.

'But that's what I am,' he said. 'A writer.'

'I thought you're a Colonel.'

'They're not mutually exclusive,' he said. 'A writer by avocation, if you will.' And then in a burst of honesty: 'But *manqué*, mind. *Manqué*. Like so much else about me. To tell you the truth I've never really got much beyond the notebook stage. Of which there are currently four. All black. Got bogged down in the preliminaries, you might say, the literary foreplay, the verbal vamping, the syntactical slap and tickle . . .' He paused, wondering how she would respond to a light illustrative slap on the knee or preferably the thigh, or a little tickle around the toes?

But judging by her blank, concentrated stare, she was not following him at all; the gesture might well be misconstrued and he could end up with more than a little slap himself and no tickle at all . . .

In fact the girl looked completely mystified. 'So what are you writing my name for?' she wanted to know.

He'd made a mistake, obviously. She wasn't Anna. She was Ahna. Not her fault, of course. But still, he'd made a mistake.

She was losing interest in any case; he could see by the way her grip had tightened on her bag, her keys. 'OK,' she said. 'I'll read it some other time then.'

He sat miserably, looking after her, but she didn't turn to look back at him, not even while she was waiting for the lift.

The truth was, no one had time for him. They all thought he was too old, beyond it. He could say anything he liked, no matter how outrageous and no one would even care. Ah, Annie,

Annie, he thought and the name really did begin to ring in his heart, to positively toll, like a death-knell, hollow, echoing . . . Where was Annie now, when he needed her?

No one cared. No one took him seriously. To prove it, to compound his misery, he caught hold of Sister Mary Bartholomew's hand before she could pick up the tea-tray.

'Sister,' he said urgently. 'My coronal sutures have parted. You will see that my brain, like a baby's, is now protected by nothing more than a thin, throbbing membrane . . .'

He put his head down and scrabbled in his hair.

'Your corona, Colonel Knoesen? Your corona?' she said doubtfully. 'You know I only work in the kitchen . . .'

'Can't you see it throbbing, throbbing . . .?'

'Throbbing? I can see dandruff jumping about like fleas,' she said. 'You're leaving a drift on the cloth.'

'What?' He couldn't believe it.

'There,' she said. 'That greyish-white drift.'

'Isn't that sugar?' he asked, amazed.

'Your eyes are going,' she pronounced. 'Why aren't you wearing your spectacles? I'll ask Sister Mary Benedict if I can get you some Gill. And then maybe Nurse Rousseau can help you wash your hair . . .'

'Nursie Thelma?' Rudy felt better at once. Little Nurse Thelma, she of the large pink ears? It was a wonderful idea. Maybe he could try his little 'piece' on her? Tell her about himself? Would she listen?

Not much point in trying Sister Mary Bartholomew. He looked at her jowly face, more than downy on the upper lip; at her thick eyebrow, straight as a die over her small blue eyes. Of course, appearances could be deceptive but the woman did look as thick as her eyebrow. And then she hadn't appreciated his throbbing corona joke either.

He gathered his papers before Sister Mary Bartholomew

could screw them up, put them on her tray and throw them out, along with the other rubbish. Not that that would have been much of a loss, really.

Rudy looked at his 'piece', turning one blank page after the other. Because that was what they were, after the quotation about de Gaulle and Anna's name. There was nothing, not a line, not a word. And that had been his point, of course, the point Ahna hadn't allowed him to make, what he had been trying to get at, his conversation piece, his considered commentary and conclusions on politics, life, everything . . . And nothing.

Annie had appreciated it when he'd placed the blank pages of his political piece before her. She'd understood and indulged him, as always. They'd concurred that the country, indeed the world, was in a parlous state, its problems way beyond any mere political solution. No doubt the politicians were aware of the insoluble nature of the ecological and economic problems, of inflation, unemployment, burgeoning populations and increasing lawlessness, of the disaffection, even alienation, of the youth, the sad lack of vision, purpose or goal.

How long then would it be before those they governed began to realise their leaders' impotence and how long before the world descended into anarchy and chaos?

How long could they go on pretending they were in control, to themselves and everyone else, when everyone, often without even knowing why, was becoming increasingly suspicious?

'We've long since passed the age of angst,' he'd told her. 'It's demoralisation now, the *Zeitgeist* of the post-modern world. And its end will be the new savagery, the ultimate and final barbarism born of despair.'

'But why didn't you put all that down?' she'd asked him. 'I mean, you were the political columnist?'

Political columnist. Had he told her that as well?

'*Schadenfreude*, must have been *schadenfreude* . . . Fact is, I wasn't the political columnist for all that long . . .'

'What?' she'd asked, frowning.

'Wait,' he'd said. 'Let me explain. This piece is, you see, more than political. It's autobiographical too, in a sense. I was laying myself quite bare. Opening up. EXPOSING myself, metaphorically speaking. I was fairly wrestling with the ineluctable at the time, pressured to produce. One deadline after the other. And me religiously apolitical. A bit of a handicap for a political columnist, don't you agree? Fact is, I hate dirty tricks, causes and ideologies. Fascists, communists, national-ists, liberals, revolutionaries. They're all the same. Jackals, all of them; opportunists. Eye to the main chance.'

She'd nodded, agreeing as usual. 'Although there are degrees. Some things are relative?' Annie had always under-stood, about words, ideas and debate, and how best to keep the real issues at bay.

'You mean,' he'd said, 'that there are degrees between the simply expedient, the frankly ruthless and the fearful liars? I think not. Hence my obeisance in de Gaulle's direction. De Gaulle was neither right nor left; de Gaulle was above. By his own admission.'

'All right. But why write my name over and over?' she'd asked, like Ahna, although much more equably.

'Because this was the ONE time I did manage to gather myself together in a quite singular effort to be collected and pointed, directed and on target. What I think I was trying to say is, THIS is the name . . .'

'De Gaulle? Or Anna?' she'd teased.

'Either. Both,' he'd said. 'Evocative, don't you think? Establishing the primary premise, wouldn't you say?'

She'd turned the blank pages. 'I still think it's a cop-out.

Why didn't you write what you've just been telling me . . . All that about the political jackals . . .?'

He shrugged. Hadn't it been done? In any case it had always been feint and parry with him. He'd never really made it to the cut and thrust. He'd long since given up hoping that what he had in the black notebooks would amount to an *oeuvre* of any sort. 'Of course,' he'd told her, 'what I really wanted to write was an entertainment, another "Pnin", something to galvanise us all into wrenching laughter, something truly cathartic . . . As Lamb pointed out, people with a speck of the motley in their make-up always have four quarters of the globe on their side. And I need that. I need to have someone on my side. Or, preferably, at my side.' He'd taken her hand. 'Maybe, like any politician, it's only acceptance that I crave?'

'Maybe,' she'd said, enigmatically.

'But I'll get it down one day, Annie,' he'd promised her. 'You remember Forster's tyranny of time and the need to tell a story? Well, I've been thinking of making some sort of obeisance in that direction . . . A simple story . . .'

But he never had. It was beyond him, carpetbagging Colonel, hornswoggling journalist, *petit bourgeois* deviationist or whatever else he had been, or pretended to be, in his time . . .

It had depressed him, talking to 'Ahna' and Sister Mary Bartholomew, and remembering Annie. He was beyond it. He'd never achieve anything now. He was too old, cold, and shivery. His life was drawing to a close and perhaps there was something portentous about having one's life draw to a close at the turn of a millennium. *Fin de siècle* and *fin de* millennium. *Mille ans.* Whatever. (Where was Annie now? She'd had more than a smattering of French.) It was as if time itself were in sympathy, winding down along with all of them there in the Home.

It had been something too, the last millennium. But how

much of it could one believe? History was written by the conquerors. Then again, how much could one know for sure even about contemporary events when they were being falsified daily by evasive politicians and partisan journalists? They even had a name for it. Disinformation. More acceptable than 'bare-faced lies', obviously.

Still, everyone knew about Hitler and Stalin, fascism and socialism. And imperialism. Western imperialism, gobbling up the globe, imposing its culture, manners and mores on everyone else. Strong enough to do so. Superior too, he supposed; militarily, anyway. And intellectually. The only one to have studied all the others systematically, after first subjugating and then liberating them. And incidentally spawning the murderously divisive nationalisms, tribalisms and genocides.

One evil leading to the next, he reflected, from the time the dying Ottoman Empire was torn apart and devoured piecemeal by the hyenas of Europe. Who then proceeded to tear each other apart in the Great War which led to the even Greater War.

It must have seemed like Armageddon, the Apocalypse itself, at least in Europe and Japan . . .

Of course, like most South Africans he, Rudy, hadn't been personally involved. Nothing much beyond rubbing shoulders with slightly drunk tommies and pommies and a few yanks in hotel bars, joining them in singing sentimental songs about meeting again, and bumming du Mauriers and C to Cs off them. The war had seemed no more than a distant storm which had washed up a tidal wave of soldiers, sailors and airmen. They had hardly impinged on his comfortable colonial existence.

In fact, the closest he personally had come to the war was to briefly entertain the notion that he could land a job as a war correspondent. But of course, jobs like that had gone to older, tougher, more experienced journalists, not pink-cheeked novices like himself.

He'd been no more than an apprentice at that time, doing the journalistic equivalent of sweeping up hair from a Salon floor, being sent from office to office with clippings, memos and assorted verbal messages, going down to the presses and up to the staff lounge, up and down, carrying this and that all day long, never putting pen to paper or finger to typewriter until, by the time they had finally given him some assignments, he'd lost interest and gone to the bioscope.

He was going to write though, he'd told them, really write. He'd been fired with ambition, and confidence. He'd be another Bosman. An urban Bosman. After all, the cities were also full of characters. Only, when he came to think about it, none of them were as droll as the Groot Maricoans. The people he knew had been Steinbeckian, Faulknerian, bordering on the Williamsian. And one had to write what one knew, even if it was the darker, Gothic side.

He had managed to get some of it down on paper, a long time ago. Nothing much more than notes at that stage, unrelated ideas and impressions, a few descriptions he had considered incisive at the time, product of a wicked, wily eye. But nothing much more than that, a few notes, and many of them lost now as well.

He'd had his best chance with Evadne. For writing, anyway. And it hadn't been too bad a life, from that point of view. Ample opportunity to write. If only he hadn't been so overwhelmed by all the opportunity . . .

And looking back now, Evadne hadn't been all that bad, either; compared with Mavis, for instance. Or Sister Mary Bartholomew.

She used to tinkle on the piano and most times it was pleasant enough, reading and pretending to write in the study while she was giving her highly iconoclastic rendering of a Chopin étude or Beethoven sonata. She'd been fond of the *Pathetique*, he remembered, and had devoted herself to wringing every last drop of pathos out of it too, lingering long and lovingly on the top E flat before sliding down the chromatic scale, oblivious of the number of notes she was missing in the process.

But occasionally, in a more tempestuous mood, she had tackled Rachmaninov, giving the dire chords such menacing power that a gloom seemed to settle on the house and he imagined it had suddenly become thronged with the shades of shock-haired composers holding their ears in dismay and even disbelief.

The trouble was that Evadne was undisciplined and unschooled musically and not too respectful of the composer's intentions and timing either. She'd used their compositions to fashion her own, as a hang-glider might use a current of air, soaring off in her own independent direction, veering here and there, slow or fast, as the mood took her.

'Interpretation', she'd called it when he'd protested the unfamiliar sound of much of her Fantasy Impromptu. 'Getting to the real heart of the thing,' she'd said, going on to explain about Ss and Gs, Specific Talents and General Intelligence, and how, if the G was in ascendance the S was not slavish but creative in itself. And that was what she was doing, re-composing the creations of Chopin, Liszt and Beethoven, which was her prerogative, he supposed, like it was her piano. Although he had noticed that the re-creations always happened to be more drastic and radical in those passages which were the more difficult to play.

She'd been an opinionated old thing, after all, as became the widow of a respected academic. Small and birdlike, she used her elbows to create the illusion of size, as some birds did by flapping and dragging their wings when challenged; not that he'd ever opposed her or asserted himself in any way. For one thing she was much older and he respected her age and experience; for another he set great store by the quiet life.

And then of course the house was hers, everything in it was hers, and the income was hers. She was supporting him while he devoted himself to his creative pursuits, researching and writing, and he was not about to ruffle her feathers in any way.

It was far too good a life, the best he'd managed to garner for himself so far and he'd intended to make it last. To that end he'd catered to her every whim, exercising his considerable charm and power of deception, flattering her at every turn, paying her the most outrageous compliments, telling her that there was no doubt about it at all, she'd improved immeasurably on Chopin, Liszt and Beethoven and he only wished they could hear how she'd managed to lick their pieces into shape, giving them the cogency and artistic validity they'd previously lacked.

'No, but really,' he'd managed to say when she'd looked at him doubtfully, small head cocked to one side like a suspicious little sparrow, beady eyes focused on his disingenuous face, hands still poised over the keyboard.

He'd managed to keep his expression both straight and disingenuous for as long as it took to convince her that he was entirely sincere, which she always allowed in the end, even if, privately, she may have thought him fatuous, or at best partial, and that was all to the good; it was a workable relationship which had to be sustained at all costs if it was going to remain workable.

Of course he had been younger in those days, and debonair; his hair had been thick and dark and he'd worn a neat goatee as well as a moustache to compensate for his overbite and the impression it gave of a rather weak chin.

He'd had more flesh on his bones too in those days, late

twenties, early thirties as he had been; a bit of muscle in the pectoral region as well. And he'd known how to be gallant, courtly even, which was it, exactly. He'd played courtier to Evadne's queen, knight errant, love-sick troubadour; and although she'd been older and a bit battered by reality, he'd managed more or less to persuade her of the viability of true romantic love and its adjunct, the happily ever after.

It had worked with Mavis as well, who had also been older and very battered indeed by both reality and her late husband the trawler captain, by the time he had come into her life fresh from the park, so to speak, from the rigours of which she had saved him, and to which she could presumably just as easily have kicked him back at any time, since they had never actually got as far as signing a marriage contract.

He'd preferred to be bound by love, he'd told her, charming her into acceptance, which wasn't too difficult, perhaps because she was a bit wary of binding legal arrangements herself, deep down.

But Evadne had been sharper than Mavis, and always trembling on the brink of disbelief it had seemed to him, of suspicion that she was being tricked in some way, only she couldn't quite put her finger on it. He'd had to work harder with her, a fact that drove him into the study to recuperate, to gather his resources before devising new, exciting and convincing ways to allay her suspicions and render her compliant and trusting again.

It had been a strain (especially when she was in her more innovative moods, musically) which was why he hadn't stayed as long as he might have if she'd been a more quiescent type, and not so sharp and prickly, a fact which no doubt contributed to his first mental breakdown (not to mention the arrest, incarceration and court case which had preceded that break-down).

Still, there had been good times too; like the holidays. Evadne had had a penchant for game, both to eat and to view, so it was off to the Kruger Park for their honeymoon and once every year after that for each of the five or so he had spent with her and her sprout, Lillith, the *fille fatale*.

He remembered the holidays with some pleasure: the clean crisp early mornings with everyone up and about before sunrise; Skukuza, the main camp, crowded with people in khaki safari gear and ankle boots. What a strange cross-cultural mix it had been, of Europe, America, the Far East and Africa, of tourist and indigene.

He remembered the bracing frontier feeling of all the camps, especially the smaller ones, like Pretoriuskop and Satara; small islands of the familiar, comprising a few rondavels, braai areas and ablution blocks, with the raw unknown beyond, where the beast was sovereign and the gawpers in their cars as alien as if they'd just come off the moon.

The starlings, at home in both worlds, having made peace with civilisation or at least having seen the advantages of an accommodation, occasioned delighted oohs and aahs as they darted around with their bright orange eyes and lustrous blue feathers, devouring the endless supply of scattered tidbits.

He'd enjoyed it all, deciding that the tourists were stranger than the game, the Germans and Japanese in particular more exotic than either buffalo or crocodile.

Evadne didn't notice the people. She'd had a fine disdain for strangers, and especially foreign strangers.

He saw her again, in her iridescent midnight blue nylon tracksuit and orange-framed sunglasses posing for photographs and looking for all the world like a starling herself; the Queen of the Starlings, or even their goddess, the way they ducked and dived and wove reverent patterns around her little black boots.

Anyway, airbrush the baggy Brits, the ever-smiling toothy Taiwanese and the amiable Americans out of the picture and what was left? Himself among the noble animals like some lordly latter-day Adam. He'd even called Evadne 'Eve' once or twice while they were there, only half joking.

Thinking again of Forster's injunction made him wonder whether that had not been his problem all along: his inability to simply tell a story, or to tell a simple story (or, perhaps, to tell a story simply?).

That had to be his trouble, because he HAD tried seriously once, during his time with Evadne (before Lillith had suddenly become nubile, or had suddenly begun to confuse him with her nubility), and he'd actually got a story down on paper. A story, moreover, that had grown into a novel, his *magnum opus*. His only *opus*, in fact.

Only it couldn't have been simple enough because the publisher hadn't been able to understand it, as the letter of rejection had indicated.

They'd had a long argument about it, the publisher and he. Hirsute fellow, Rudy remembered, bushy hair and beard; but then he'd always been sensitive to hair, relic of his childhood spent in the Salon, listening to the Professor of Tonsorial Artistics expound on the desirability of a neatly trimmed head.

He'd tried to explain while the publisher kept looking at his watch, with his blue eyes round and antagonistic behind his horn-rimmed spectacles.

'I was excavating, probing, laying out a trench,' he'd said, terribly angry that explanations should have been necessary. But of course he'd been young then. One lost the capacity to become really angry as one grew older, maybe because everything mattered less and less . . . 'That's a metaphor by the way.'

Unblinking blue eyes peered out at him from under the bushy hair. Totally unsympathetic.

'It's a family saga, don't you see, but it's a metaphor for . . . Oh, don't you see, Matthew and Tony and Hendrickje. They're quarter-brothers. They wear white ducks and fair-isles in the teeth of the jeans and T-shirt revolution. Sartorial counter-insurgents. Rag-trade revisionists.'

'Quarter-brothers?' the publisher had asked faintly, as if it really were too much for him, having to keep his temper, his patience, to remain more or less polite, while he, Rudy, was simmering and seething, clenching his fists, grinding his teeth, drawing great shuddering breaths, trying not to hyperventilate too much in the effort to remain similarly patient and polite and in control.

'One of them has another father and his wife only wet-nursed him.'

'That's Matthew?'

'You DO understand,' he had exclaimed, instantly willing to forgive the man for everything, for his patronising tone and attitude, his insufferable air of superiority, his power-play, the fact that he had all the advantages, held all the cards . . .

'It's about relationships, you see, artistic, creative interplay, influences and connections, not always healthy, of course; I mean, Hendrickje Stoffels on Rembrandt's knee, Wordsworth and Dorothy too in a way . . .'

He was becoming very excited. They were waiting for him at home, Evadne and Lillith, waiting to hear the good news, that the rejection had been a mistake, that he'd been able to explain, to convince.

'Rembrandt's knee. I didn't get that. Nothing seemed to follow on, if you know what I mean.'

He'd had to impress the fellow somehow, make him believe that only he hadn't been up to understanding it. The Emperor's new clothes tactic. 'You will see, when you come to read it carefully, that I deliberately limited the arbitrariness of incident in order to preserve the illusion of mystery.'

'That's exactly it! As I said, it's so mysterious no one knows what you're talking about . . .'

'Well then,' Rudy had said, a deathly calm coming over him, speaking through his tightly clenched teeth. 'What you don't understand is the distillation of nearly half a lifetime of observation, my considered commentary and conclusions . . .'

But he wasn't even listening, he'd just gone straight on: '. . . full of neologisms no one can decipher. You've written in some sort of code to which only you have the key!'

He'd given up then. He'd gripped the desk and leaned over, his knuckles white, trying to get right into the publisher's face.

'Well, let me tell you something! If you don't have your hair, moustache and beard trimmed soon you're going to look like you're wearing a balaclava! And I happen to have an eminently sound trichological background! In fact, you're seriously disadvantaged, labiomantically speaking! And there's a neologism for you to put in your pipe and smoke!'

Childish, of course; but better than breaking down and weeping on the man's desk.

Evadne and Lillith were waiting for him when he got home, confident that he would have been able to make his case, explain himself. They rushed to greet him, reminding him of that special feeling in a household on a wedding afternoon when the dogs and the children somehow sense that the usual constraints don't apply and they're everywhere, underfoot, generating excitement. And then the let-down: the wedding is off, the bridegroom has snuffed it, return the presents, take the champagne off the ice . . .

Of course he'd been a fool. One didn't do that sort of thing. One didn't try to explain oneself to a publisher. He'd betrayed himself, betrayed his position as the de Gaulle of the literary world, above acceptance or rejection. A measure of his desperation. Evadne had after all believed that his novel would be a *tour de force* . . .

Which made him wonder: what had happened to it? Mislaid between the house and the jail perhaps. Thrown out with everything he hadn't been able to pack. Burnt, probably. Evadne would have wanted to erase any trace of him after she'd laid the charge of molestation and he had gone to jail.

Remembering the jail episode reminded him of the reason for his going to ground in the park the first time with Muddy Waters, Pypsie and the others: bilking. On the lam from the law. Scared spitless of being sent to a Work Colony. And when one lacked the resources to get really far away, to the Seychelles, the Bahamas, Chile, or somewhere like that, the park and the bush were the only alternatives. Although there had been times, he had to admit, especially when it rained and the water got in everywhere, dripping down on him from the trees, tipped into his shoes from the reeds, that the Colony HAD seemed preferable, but only sometimes . . .

As always when his thoughts began to distress him, Rudy sought to escape, but in the Home his options were severely limited. There was only his little room – where, sitting or lying all alone, the memories would come crowding in, especially the ones that made him cringe with shame and pain – or the lounge, where he could listen to the others reminisce, a viable alternative, he had come to realise. Other people's memories were neither painful nor shameful . . .

He listened to them, not wanting to be drawn in but needing to be distracted.

'. . . Chinese take-aways and pastries left over from the parish tea-party, the best they could do for my seventy-third . . .'

'. . . doing the Lambeth Walk, oy!'

' . . . and I said, "Well, what about a spot then?" '

'All thumbs and elbows, ducked when he saw the ball coming, never made it on to the team, not even the reserves . . .'

'. . . and the Palais Glide, right there in the foyer!'

'. . . results coming over the loudspeaker from the Oosterlig, the Nats going bananas in the streets!'

'Ah, Scotland! That garret of the earth, that knuckle-end of Britain, that land of Calvin, oat-cakes and sulphur . . .' Rudy burst out, apropos of nothing, but that was the way of it, in that place, conversations were a collage of weird inconsequentialities.

'What? What was that about Scotland?' Neville McNaughton asked, beginning to go red in the face. 'I'm of Scottish descent, I'll have you know . . .'

'Nothing more than that, really,' Rudy said mildly. 'Sydney Smith. Nineteenth-century clergyman-critic. To give credit where it's due. And take some myself, for remembering all that.'

'That's the trouble with you,' Neville grumped. 'Never understand what you're getting at . . .'

'Like Alistair,' Edna Something-or-Other said. 'Mysterious.'

'People have said that about me before,' Rudy said, surprised to discover that now, at the end of his life, he was beginning to derive a perverse satisfaction from the fact that no one – with the possible exception of Annie – had ever understood him. It was something, an accomplishment of sorts, to have gone through a whole long life so thoroughly, so consistently misunderstood . . .

SEVEN

FITTING IN

In his search for congenial company Rudy followed Lyle Hargood and Neville McNaughton to the bench in the garden which looked out over the bay.

They'd made a joke about having to get away from the 'old hens' for a bit, but it was a fine day and the sea was always a talking point.

'It's never the same, have you noticed?' Rudy said. 'When the sun comes up, those bands of vermilion reflected on the water; polka dots sometimes when there are holes in the clouds.'

'Polka dots!' Neville snorted.

'And rays of light coming down like rain.'

'I like that,' Lyle said. 'I've always liked words, books.'

'Bit of a paedophile myself,' Rudy said, and then, appalled at the slip, Freudian as it may have been, he drew a sharp breath. 'Bibliophile, I meant to say, of course . . .'

'You can have it for me,' Neville grumped.

'What? Bibliophilia?'

'The SEA. Thought we're talking about the sea.'

'The sea . . .' Lyle said dreamily. 'The Colonel's right, you know. Sometimes there is only one hole in the clouds and then the sun beams down like a spotlight on the water.'

'That's it,' Rudy said. He liked Lyle. The man was a bit obsessive, even daft, as Neville said, but articulate at least and lucid most of the time; he had all his faculties, and that was something in that place.

'And sometimes the clouds form little arabesques like a white lace curtain above the blue . . .' Lyle was saying. 'But it's not just blue, is it? Blue is too banal. Azure, perhaps, aqua-marine, sapphire, or cerulean . . .'

'Not when you're in it like we were, mate,' Neville said, 'torpedoed in mid-Atlantic like that, lucky to be alive. Divine retribution, I've always thought, because Sodom had nothing on that boat. Living like bums, most of them.'

'Bums?' Rudy tittered, wondering what they were in for.

'Had my points of honour, though. And there were some decent chaps amongst them.'

'I know a bit about that,' Rudy offered.

Neville looked at him with interest. 'Where exactly did you see service then?'

'No, I mean, I know a bit about living like a bum. Preferred that to carting sheets of paper upstairs and down; which was why I was on my smiling old uppers, most of the time . . .' Because what did it matter if they knew, after all? Those were episodes in a long full life, something to talk about (unlike some of the other episodes in his life . . .). In fact, looking back on it, some periods of his life had begun to assume quite a romantic cast; he'd been part of the sixties, after all. It had been *de rigueur*, almost, to drop out, to hit the road – the first time he'd done so, anyway . . .

'Never sailed myself. Trouble with the old inner ear, you know. Lovely to watch, though, very early, when the ships are silhouetted against the horizon like cardboard cut-outs . . .'

'You're daft, Hargood,' Neville said. 'That's your trouble.'

They were like a comic turn, Rudy thought. Like Laurel and Hardy. Old McNaughton, big and choleric as they came, and little Lyle Hargood with his mild manner and dreamy eyes.

'And after the war?' Rudy asked. 'What did you do?'

'Met a cherry and started a little business. Rubber stamps, cutting keys, gifts, that sort of thing . . . married her too.'

'A cherry? You mean, an Indian girl?'

'INDIAN girl? What Indian girl?' Neville's red face turned purple. Threatening a seizure, Rudy thought, at the very least. But somehow he couldn't take it seriously. Neville might fall down gasping, eyes bulging, but in the very next instant he would bounce up again, like Hardy . . .

'I thought a "cherry" was an Indian girl,' Rudy said. 'Not that it matters. Not illegal any more, you know. Perfectly acceptable. Even preferable, sometimes. Very affirmative. I mean, I was quite friendly myself, once, with a person of colour,' he said, thinking of Zolah. 'And when THAT association became unappetising as . . . cold pumpkin, I moved on again. To the other side of town. Only I was too old for it by then. Nearly died that time. And by the time they pulled me in here I was nothing more than a walking splint, as my old acquaintance Gladstone used to say. Spiky as an aloe. Very Shavian . . .'

'You're as daft as he is,' Neville grumped.

'It's getting hot out here,' Lyle murmured.

'Call this hot!' Neville exploded, as if on cue. 'I can tell you about hot. AND cold. Fifty degrees plus to well below zero. And if that wasn't bad enough you could always get lost, disoriented in the sandstorms, flaying wind, grit everywhere. Sink down for a minute and you're just another dune.'

'Could we move over into the shade?' Lyle persisted.

'AND if you're lucky enough to reach the bivouac you're

blistered all over, even under your nails . . . The Colonel will know. Whereabouts were you stationed?' he asked Rudy suddenly.

Taken by surprise, Rudy blurted out: 'Uh . . . Samarkand. Or somewhere near there. On the Golden Road. Or a track a few miles south anyway. In a wadi. I used to sift the sand through my fingers and wonder how they live, those nomads, Bedouins, whatever. They were always there, you know, appearing, then melting back into the desert, waiting for us to weaken. Like vultures, in their long flapping garments. After our weapons I imagine. Tuaregs a bit different. They're of Berber extraction, you know, fine features. Caucasian. Impressive sight on their camels, the men veiled, sporting rather elegant silver jewellery and amber in their hair. You want to get invited to their three small cups of tea ceremony, something like the Japanese . . . I never got that far though, mixing socially . . .'

Neville's eyes were bulging. 'Sitting in a wadi? Didn't you see action?' he blustered.

'There was an encounter,' Rudy said. 'A sort of minor skirmish . . .'

'Skirmish! You're pulling my leg? He's pulling my leg,' he told Lyle.

'Not at all. There I was, on the sand, in the sand, sand all over, just as you said, under my nails, trying to remember what good moist brown earth felt like, telling the flies to shag off, when we saw them file past, three long columns, all bound up in mummifying bandages. The officer looked straight at me. Big fiery eyes he had, burning out of his bandages like fog lamps.'

'Well, what were they then? Arabs? Huns? Itis?'

'Brits,' Rudy said. 'I thought they were Brits.'

'And what did he say, the officer?' Lyle asked.

'He had some gripe or other,' Rudy said. 'I can't remember

what.' But they were both looking so expectantly at him that he felt obliged to continue: 'He said, well, he said . . . something along the lines of, a household name one week, out on your slippery arse the next, brainwashed by big business, raped by the almighty dollar, rendered down by country club digestive juices until there's nothing left of you but your hacking jacket, your hunting-stock and your haw-haw-haw . . . Something like that, and all in a broad Anglo-Indian accent. Might have mentioned "shooting stick" as well. Quoting somebody, I should think. Out of a book, or a film, maybe. Sounded familiar anyway. But I don't know what they were. Not Brits, exactly, except for the officer, perhaps. King's Indian Rifles maybe. Sikhs, I think, all shot to hell, something like that . . .'

They subsided for a while, wondering about him, Rudy could tell, until Lyle said: 'I've heard the desert can be like the sea, always changing. The colours too, mauve and pink as the sun comes up, turning to copper and gold.'

'Sweated my guts out in that desert,' Neville huffed. 'Gypo guts, and boils all over. I never sat in a bloody wadi playing with the sand and watching the sun come up. Or the caravans go by. And then when we got back what did we get? What did YOU get?'

'Nothing,' Rudy said truthfully. 'I never got anything.'

'Exactly.'

'Prefer the sea, I think,' Lyle offered. 'Especially at night when the chokka boats are strung out across the horizon like fairy-lights . . .'

'Fairy-lights! Well you should know,' Neville grunted. 'What was your game, then, after the war?' he asked Rudy.

'Did all sorts of things really,' Rudy said. 'Worked with a pathologist for a while; Swiss fellow called Gorman, carving up cadavers behind frosted window-panes.'

'Cadavers!'

'It was a living,' Rudy shrugged. 'And one of the more respectable things I've done. Profitable too. Only I couldn't take the smell. Of death, you know. Sickly sweet. And the pungent odour of the formalin . . .'

'Let's get off that then.'

'What? Pathology?'

'Death. Enough of that around here.'

Which was true, of course. Rudy didn't mind. Too much of a strain anyway, sifting through it all, separating fact from fiction, or trying to . . . Because there really had been a Swiss pathologist called Gorman; he of the thick beard and thicker accent, according to Gladstone, his old bunkmate in the Work Colony. Gladstone had had endless stories to tell about Gorman and his friend, Herr Reeper, also a pathologist, who'd blown his mind and wore a screwed-down skull which impaired his hearing. Still heard music, though, and had the tonic sol-fa lined up, from a spleen in a specimen beaker to a tonsil in a test-tube. Although it may have been a testicle, Gladstone wasn't sure. 'Do you mean,' Rudy had asked him, 'that they look the same?' 'In formalin, exactly,' Gladstone had said. Anyway Herr Reeper had been able to ping out a flat but recognisable rendition of Deutschland Über Alles with his bistoury. Sounded like a glockenspiel, apparently.

Rudy had been intrigued. He would have liked to assemble his own tonic sol-fa, if only human parts hadn't been so difficult to come by. In honour of Gladstone in a way, and something to remember him by.

He'd retold Gladstone's stories countless times. He'd even committed some of them to his black notebooks; amongst the few things he'd actually got down – not counting the cryptic novel – and they weren't even his own stories, nothing he could take credit for. But who could he acknowledge, after all? Not an unknown tramp called Gladstone (on the distaff side, he used to say, one of the bends sinister, and he was, one could see at first glance, quite seriously bent) who was probably dead and buried anyway, or rotting somewhere, since so civilised an end as burial may not have been his lot, unless the state had taken a hand in it and thrown his remains into the proverbial unmarked hole in the ground.

Feelings had been running high for some time. There had been whisperings in the passages, heated discussions in the doorways of rooms; a concerted grumble was rising up from the place. The low-pitched moan continued from the frail-care sections, but the grumble almost overtook it at times.

A welcome relief, really, Rudy felt. Any change made for some excitement, although he hadn't really wanted to be drawn in. It was about the chairs, ostensibly, but actually they were all needing to blow off some steam, and the chairs were no more than a pretext.

Everyone knew that, the Sisters included. It happened from time to time, on one issue or another: the food – which was passable, he felt, lacking in colour and variety and flavour sometimes, mainly because so little salt was used, but edible; being woken up for tea at five; having supper at five and not being able to watch TV after eight; all these grievances had engaged them in turn and they had had meetings with Mother Mary Therese playing the game with them, giving each an opportunity to moan and complain and threaten and accuse one another of this and that, and in the end Mother Mary Therese always explained why nothing could be changed.

Legitimate explanations, of course: not so much salt because it wasn't good for one, likewise spices of any sort; the black staff had to catch buses and taxis and had to leave by six; the TV created disturbances, etc etc, and so things stayed exactly as they had always been, but everyone dispersed feeling much better. They had expressed their opinions, they had voiced their preferences, they were important, they had been listened to, they had got rid of all their pent-up resentments and life could go on again.

But the issue of the chairs had cropped up before, apparently, and it involved the best seats in the lounge always going to those who could walk faster, or had less to do than the others.

Initially some of them had laid claim to special chairs, but there had been so much fuss if anyone dared to sit on a 'booked' chair that Mother Mary Therese had ruled that the chairs belonged to the Home and first come, first served. This resulted in a mad scramble to get to the lounge first after every meal when the lucky ones would sit, triumphant and immovable, in the best chairs.

Rudy never joined in this sprint because he couldn't abide rushing through his meals, so by the time he made his leisurely entrance there was nothing left for him to sit on but the old fraying wicker chair no one else had wanted.

Teeth came into it as well: a few still had their own teeth and could go directly to the lounge after meals; others had dentures and had to go back to their rooms first to rinse them or they would have to spend most of the day putting up with the discomfort of crumbs and other irritants under their bridgework. Like oysters, as someone complained.

Rudy was the only one who laughed at that and they had all stared at him, scandalised by his lack of appreciation of the gravity of the matter.

But that was unfair. The old wicker chair had bits of cane sticking up and a cushion so depleted as to consist of little more than its cover. He was in wholehearted agreement with them. The matter was grave all right.

'We could take turns,' Vera Myles suggested. 'Draw up a roster'.

She was immediately challenged by Joey who wanted to know why SHE, Vera, always got the little fold-up table for her cards, 'because that's not fair.'

The fold-up table wasn't the issue just then, but Rudy could see them making a mental note that there was only one fold-up table and that could well become an issue in the future because it wasn't fair, was it?

'That's what it's all about,' someone else offered. 'Fairness.'

That was what it was all about. Only, who would keep the roster? Mother had seen her opportunity. It would be complicated. The staff didn't have time, the Sisters didn't have time. No one volunteered.

'A few more cushions, fatter cushions,' Rudy offered. 'That's all. A good cushion and there'll be nothing to choose between them. The chairs, that is.'

'It isn't,' someone objected at once. The meeting had hardly got under way. They couldn't possibly come to any sort of conclusion yet, especially not one as simple and obvious as that.

'Colonel Knoesen is right,' Mother Mary Therese pronounced. 'I'll ask Father Lacey to make an appeal to the congregation on Sunday. I'm sure the people would be only too pleased, everyone's got old cushions lying around . . .'

'It isn't only that,' someone else complained. 'It's the backs as well. Some of them have good backs, good support. Others get you in the ribs, or the spine, most uncomfortable.'

'It's the government,' Neville said, banging his stick. 'Cutting grants and subsidies, that's what they're doing.'

'Always got a knife in for the government,' Vera Myles said. 'Good old Mac.'

'Mac the Knife.'

Some of them began to laugh. The tension was defused. The meeting was over.

'I'll see about the cushions,' Mother promised, relieved that it had ended so amicably, with everyone more or less satisfied.

'They can laugh, but most people don't know what happened,' Neville told Rudy. 'When we got back from up north, the government . . .'

'But that was another government.'

'Governments are all the same, given time, just you wait . . .'

Mother was the last to leave, the Sisters having drifted off as soon as the issue was resolved.

'How many cushions?' she asked.

They all got up and the counting of the cushions took up a good few minutes, pleasurable minutes, judging from the jokes about tender tails, bony bottoms, and suchlike.

Every loose cushion in the room was taken up to be minutely examined, thrown up to gauge the weight, pummelled to gauge the springiness or otherwise and counted, with the final number, after much argument about the borderline cushions, given to Mother Mary Therese.

After that they settled down again. Vera Myles went back to laying out her cards. Edna Something (had they said Simpson or Simpkins when she was introduced?) started moaning about Alistair and Joey about her sisters.

The new arrival, Sybil, who was stinking rich and childless (unless they'd said childish?), seemed to be looking curiously at him so Rudy half rose with a courtly bow and smiled his sweet smile. But there was no response, not even a nod of acknowledgement. He was trying to come up with a suitable remark, something with which to arouse her interest, to impress her, but before he could think of anything Joey had piped up on the other side:

'I always wondered about that cape because old Swanepoel had given it to her. I can see him as clear as day, with his salt and pepper bristles in the folds where his razor couldn't reach. She used to giggle about it which made me wonder, even if it was only second-hand . . .'

'Youngsters like myself,' Neville began telling him, 'wanted to see the world, what did we know? Smuts won THAT argument, and poor old Hertzog bought it. What did he care about the Commonwealth? Should have been the other way around.'

'What?' Rudy asked, keeping his eye on Sybil. 'What should have been the other way around?'

'We'd all have been Nationalists, that's what. Never cared about the common man. Conciliation isn't a POLICY, you know. Shouldn't be.'

'You've lost me,' Rudy said.

'I said, didn't give a tinker's damn about the common man. About the soldiers going belly up in the desert. Not then, not now. Sounds good, you know, conciliation policy, but it'll never work. Government needs to be told.'

'They'll listen to us,' Rudy said wryly.

'What's that?'

Neville's bright red cheeks were mapped with blue veins, he noticed. High blood pressure. He'd have to be careful with the man.

'Jokes aside, though, where exactly did you see service? I mean, I don't remember Samarkand . . .'

'Tell you all about it one day,' Rudy said. 'Samarkand, the bazaars of Aleppo . . .'

'The bazaars! You were in the Secret Service then!'

'Something like that,' Rudy said, trying to remember more bits and pieces from *Beau Geste*, *Lawrence of Arabia*, the *Four Feathers* and anything else that came to mind. 'Ah, those were the days. The forties. White lisle stockings, bangs and sweeps . . . page-boys and snoods . . .'

'Bangs and sweeps? You're talking HAIR?' Neville threw up his hands. 'What are you, a bloody pansy? Always wondered about Hargood, but . . . although I suppose when it comes to the Secret Service . . .'

Rudy gave up on the conversation. Neville was the confrontational sort. High colour, short fuse. He didn't want to get embroiled in anything disagreeable. He'd try Sybil again, presently . . .

'SHE said she only kissed him,' Joey was saying.

'Kissed who?' Sybil asked.

She'd pencilled her eyebrows to look like question marks, Rudy noticed. No wonder she looked curious all the time. He'd have to do something about it if anything developed between them. Couldn't live with question marks day in and day out. He'd take her out of the Home too, get her to buy them a comfortable townhouse somewhere, engage a few servants to clean and cook . . . He'd get hold of his divorce papers, make it legal, take good care of her in her declining years . . .

'Luckily she passed on, before it came to that, or we would've had old Swanepoel on our hands, only they took the lot, cut the dresses off at the top to make skirts for the house and used the bloomers and vests for dusters.'

Joey lapsed into silence and Edna Something-or-Other took up the litany: 'Didn't want to see him, not then, hid under the bed when he came around. Nobody liked him any more, nobody could stand Alistair . . .'

'Lush,' Lyle said to no one in particular. 'All around there of course, luxuriant . . . but where we were . . . it was like Eden.'

'Still got it then, have you?' Rudy asked with interest. 'The nursery?'

Lyle turned to look sadly at him. 'Didn't I tell you? About that snaky fellow?'

'That snaky fellow?'

'That snaky fellow!' Neville whooped, banging his stick. 'You're a right rum lot, you are!'

'I call him that,' Lyle said defensively, 'because when I shook his hand it was cold. His skin was rough, almost scaly, and his eyes very green. He had jet black hair smooth and shiny as a helmet. There was something about him, an aura, something ancient . . .'

'Good grief,' Rudy said. 'And what did he do? Seduce your mother?' He had spoken flippantly, intending to make a joke, but Lyle turned away from him at once.

'Seduced his mother! What next?' Neville snorted.

Neville was right, Rudy thought. They were a rum lot. No doubt about it. As rum as they could get.

With Lyle silenced Neville started up again: 'Dividing the country between the Nats and the Saps, that's what started it.'

'Who's a sap then, Oupa?' Nursie Thelma Rousseau asked with a smile.

She'd come to help with serving the tea, since it was just on teatime, the meeting having taken up so much of the morning. A sweet girl, Rudy decided, even if her ears were big and pink, like a little rabbit.

'When are you going to give my hair another wash, Nursie?' he asked. 'With Gill?'

'Colonel,' she said seriously, 'once is enough, you've got so few hairs.'

'Shame on you,' he said. 'Don't you even want to check, to see if once was enough?'

'I'm telling you,' Neville insisted. 'Dividing the country between the boers and the rooineks . . .'

'History isn't my field, exactly,' Rudy said. 'Although I have read a bit about . . . Atatürk. Did you know that he approved modern dancing, except for the Charleston and the Black Bottom which he said militated against the veil, the harem and the fez?'

'Britain gave him a chance to act on the world stage.'

'Who? Atatürk?'

Neville's face grew very red. 'What bloody Turk are you talking about?' he exploded.

'Oupa!' Nursie Thelma warned. 'Calm down. You'll get a stroke.'

'SMUTS!' Neville shouted. 'The Conciliation Policy. But it wasn't SOUTH AFRICANISM, was it?'

What was the use of trying? Rudy wondered. Neville didn't converse. He pontificated, following his own obscure train of thought.

'. . . hypnotic speech,' Lyle suddenly started up again as if he'd never been miffed: 'you know, a slight impediment, hardly a stammer, it was just barely there, an almost imperceptible hesitation on the esses, making them slightly more sibilant. A little hissss, like a snake . . .'

Joey's voice rose, drowning him out: '. . . and then I had no one but Molly and the baby and they're as good as dead for all I ever see of them . . .'

'Such sad stories,' Nursie Thelma said. 'Doesn't somebody have something happy to say?'

They all stared at her, thinking hard, but it seemed that just then, no one had.

'Well here comes tea anyway,' she said. 'That will cheer you up, hey?'

Tea always did cheer them up, and so did visitors. Some of them had quite large, devoted, or at least dutiful families, people who came to visit, who called them by name, people to whom they really were a Daddy or Grandad, a Mom or Ouma.

Not that Rudy blamed the staff for depersonalising them. Hundreds of old people spent their last few months or years there. They were in transit, so to speak, here today and gone tomorrow, so what was the point of learning names, or getting to know people, or even listening to them? It was in one ear, out the other, like with Joey now, going on about the Depression and the Sally Army again:

'. . . cardboard box full of clothes, I can still see it, clear as a photo, pulling things out, trying them on, Madgie waltzing around in a taffeta skirt right down to her ankles . . .'

She was talking to old Sybil, who looked nonplussed; but then she usually did, with those eyebrows of hers. What would she know about it anyway, wealthy old widow that she was, never known a day's want in her life, never even had children . . . What would she know about the Great Depression, or any kind of depression? Wouldn't know a box of old clothes from the back of a horse, she wouldn't.

Rudy stared speculatively at her. Apart from the eyebrows, she hadn't too bad a face; better than Mave's, at any rate, who'd had a face like a boot.

Sybil had a well-bred sort of face, too much dead white powder perhaps, and bright pink lipstick smeared all over the place. Barbara Cartlandish, in a way, and hopefully just as rich . . .

Who'd she be leaving her lot to, he wondered; any nieces, nephews? Not that he could or would ask. In any case she'd got her nose stuck into her newspaper again. A good nose though, he'd noticed. A good, straight, no-nonsense nose.

Joey had given up on Sybil and turned her attention to Vera Myles who sat at her card table shuffling and cutting, her eyes glazed. Cataracts forming, Rudy thought. And why not? They seemed to have everything else, from trench mouth to foot rot.

'There was a nearly new black velvet dress with a big red rose on the shoulder, only we never went to parties, so we hawked it around, Madgie and me, and got a shilling in the end, which was worth something in those days, you could buy a whole bolt of *crêpe de Chine*, or voile, with only a few thick threads and knots here and there . . .'

Nursie Thelma was preparing to soak Vera Myles' feet in a basin of warm water which she'd pushed under the small folding table, before trimming her ingrowing toenails. 'Is that so, Oumatjie?' she said.

But it meant nothing to her, Rudy could see that; *crêpe de Chine*, or voile . . . Denim was what they went for, these days.

He shifted uncomfortably in his chair. He'd been late getting to the lounge as usual and the chairs which still had some stuffing to them had been taken. He'd lost weight and his bones were pushing through his backside; he was bating and dwindling again, sitting on his bare bones.

'When are the new cushions coming?' he asked. 'I'm sitting on nothing but my bare bones. That's all I've got to sit on, I swear . . .'

'Voile with little green leaves . . .'

'You're soft,' Neville said. 'Couldn't have been in the desert, not the REAL desert, or you'd be cured like me. Like old leather. Have to wash myself with saddle soap . . .' He threw his head back to laugh and fell to coughing, spluttering and hawking instead.

'No, sies!' Nursie Thelma exclaimed. 'You spit on me Grandpa!'

'Apologies. Inadvertent!' Lyle offered.

'Not you, Grandpa. Him!'

'I just don't want anybody to go picking through my things when I die,' Joey said. 'Not you or anybody!'

'Picking through your things?' Sybil asked, her question marks going right up her forehead.

Her newspaper had slipped down and Rudy snatched it up before anyone else could get to it. 'Do you mind, Sybil, my

123

dear?' he asked. 'Do like to keep abreast, as much as I can.'

'After you then,' Neville said to him.

'She always had an excuse for not going to church,' Joey rambled on. 'Like her stockings were laddered.'

'Whose stockings, Oumatjie?' Nursie Thelma asked.

She'd dried Vera Myles' feet and was sitting on the floor almost under the folding table, trying to cut the toenails, still hard as horn despite the soaking, while Vera yelped and squirmed.

'We used to draw black lines down the backs of our legs to look like stocking seams. Used to darken our eyelids with pencil lead.'

'Lead?' Sybil said doubtfully.

'You know, LEAD! Got a hiding but she went on doing it.'

'That's enough now!' Vera Myles screeched suddenly, shaking her foot.

'Making lines with the lead. What I've been telling you about!'

'Oh, the lead.' Sybil was feeling all around her chair and underneath for her newspaper.

'I must do it,' Nursie Thelma pleaded. 'You don't want to get me in trouble?'

'I'll do it myself then,' Vera snapped.

'But you won't. You know you won't.'

'Howard Hughes never cut his,' Rudy said, peering out from behind the paper. 'They grew out twisted like corkscrews.'

'Mr . . . uh . . . is that my paper?' Sybil asked, question marks riding high.

'I read about that too,' Neville said. 'He used to pee in jars. Had a roomful of them . . .'

'Excuse me?' Sybil sniffed.

'You could do worse than the Salvation Army,' Joey told her.

'Actually I'm C of E,' Sybil said.

'Non-conformist, aren't they?' Rudy asked.

'C of E?' Neville snorted. 'What are you then, a bloody Roman?'

'Shhhhh,' Nursie Thelma said. She got up, rather gracefully, Rudy thought, bringing her legs forward and levering herself up slowly. Nice legs too. Pretty little thing, even if she did have those big pink ears.

Joey tried to grab hold of Sister Mary Benedict's hand as she passed. 'I want you to promise me,' she pleaded.

'On and on,' Sybil said. 'I don't rightly know what she's running on about this morning! And I'll have my paper back, if you please, Mr . . . uh . . .'

'Colonel,' Rudy said, offering her the paper with a flourish. 'Colonel R K Knoesen. Rudy to my friends.'

'It was in that magazine,' Neville said. 'All that about Howard Hughes and the jars of pee.'

'The what?' Sister Mary Benedict exclaimed, turning around to squint balefully at him. 'I'll be washing your mouth out with soap in a minute, my man, see if I don't!'

'You'll have to use saddle soap, Sister,' Rudy chuckled.

'Hours and hours, trying to explain about the Depression,' Joey complained. 'And she doesn't even try to understand. Will YOU see that nobody comes picking through my things? The Salvation Army must get it all.'

Sister Mary Benedict pursed her lips in mild disapproval before she pronounced: 'The church has some very worthy charities too, you know, but of course the choice is yours . . .'

'I just don't want anyone using my bloomers for dusters when I'm gone . . .'

Was that it? Rudy wondered. Did it really come down to that in the end? Had Joey had some sort of premonition? Maybe it was a good sign that he hadn't begun to worry about what would happen to his underwear after he'd gone?

The thought made him smile, and Lyle, catching his eye just then, smiled back. Lyle was all right, he thought. He'd be the one to cultivate if he hadn't been a man. Less of a bore than Neville, at any rate.

Still, old Sybil might be worth it. Eighty if she was a day. And rich. Couldn't do any harm. He'd taken up with worse in his time . . .

EIGHT

DOZING OFF

After lunch there was time for a doze, or dozy retrospections, the one leading to the other and so interconnected sometimes that Rudy didn't know whether he was dreaming or reminiscing. About that maddening little girl, too often, wondering whether she had been aware of the effect she was having on him as she vamped and simultaneously flaunted her lisping innocence. And that had been it exactly, that teasing paradox, that tantalising contradiction. Not quite flirting. Not exactly. But if she had been aware of the effect she was having on him, the innocence would have been simulated, wouldn't it; her exultant KNOWING, cunningly concealed?

Verboten, of course. He had known that. He wasn't, couldn't have been, that depraved. Could he?

Not that he had done anything. Evadne had become jealous of his relationship with Lillith, that was all. Or had she read his mind? Maybe the Queen of the Starlings with her sharp darting eyes had been more perspicacious than he had given her credit for.

Had it really been there, though, the coquetry? Or had Lillith merely been responding to the sick fantasy he was imposing on her?

And what had the coquetry amounted to? Dressing skimpily (or hardly at all) when he was around. Striking casually provocative poses, or sitting – as her mother used to scold her – in an unladylike way, exposing certain erogenous parts of her anatomy, or parts that he had found erotic, anyway.

But how would she have known that? Known which parts would particularly tickle his fantasy? Her thighs, for instance, covered as they were in a fine blonde down . . .

If thoughts counted he had been a dirty young man all right. He'd have to admit it; which was more than most young men would do, because they were all the same, weren't they, party to the global conspiracy, the façade of decency and decorum.

Evadne couldn't have suspected anything. He'd gone out of his way to be hard on the girl when her mother was around; but she'd seemed to have understood that as well – wise beyond her years.

Or was that the game she had played with him? Presenting her little round rump for his stepfatherly correction, wearing nothing more than tight nylon briefs, the very briefest of nylon briefs. And hadn't she asked for the loving, lingering little smacks, time after time, with her cheeky, provocative remarks? Insisting on it, almost.

And what of the elaborate shows of affection? All the hugs and squeezes?

Lillith, little Lill. Her very name with its built-in coquettish lisp had undone him, and he'd lost it completely. Pursuing the unattainable. Dreaming the impossible dream. Lillith like a doll with her blonde locks, dark blue eyes and thick, spiky lashes . . .

With Evadne it had been something else. Evadne was security, comfort. Life with Evadne had been good enough.

They'd eaten well, pudding every day and tea in bed in the mornings, served by Evadne's faithful retainer, Ducky, short for Duchess, as he'd discovered later, and not because of the way she waddled, splay-footed, when she walked.

Evadne had paid all their bills, privileged to do so, as she'd often said, when scruples had arisen (as they had on occasion but for reasons other than she imagined). When, for instance, the rigours of being married to her had seemed too big a price to pay for the comfort of her home, and even the opportunity to write for the first time in his life, of being able to give himself wholly to his work, such as it was, without financial restraints of any kind.

Sad that in spite of the most propitious arrangement he'd ever been able to make he'd had so little to show for it. Nothing beyond that one mysterious novel.

It had been pathetic. The real pieces of that time, the pieces about Lillith, had stayed in his head. One couldn't bruit that sort of thing abroad. He knew that. It had to be his secret. His, and Lillith's, Lillith with her bold, overlarge blue eyes, old beyond her years, beyond his, too, he sometimes thought, the way she'd come into her late father's study, drop her school bag, flop down with a 'Whew! Hi!' and slowly begin to strip off her black stockings, gym skirt pushed right up, spending far too long staring at him while she fiddled with the suspenders.

'What's for lunch?' she'd ask.

'You,' he'd wanted to say.

Pitiable. Pathetic cowardly young man. Worse even than a dirty old man.

He'd pretend to be writing and she'd come up behind him, lean over to read, her sharp little chin burrowing into his shoulder.

'Is this it then? The *magnum opus*?' With her delicious little gurgling giggle.

Would that it had been. He had it in his head, as always, but getting it down on paper was something else.

Something always happened in the pipeline between thought and execution. A blockage of one kind or another. Name of Lillith, little Lill, at that time.

And that was the dilemma. The opportunity had been there – courtesy of Evadne – but the distraction had been too great, also courtesy of Evadne, in a way.

So he'd have had to leave. Leave Lillith. And try to write. Or stop trying to write and have Lillith. And go to jail.

That was the dilemma.

In the end he'd stayed; for the books, he told himself. The study was full of them, the personal collection of her late husband, the Dean, all lovingly chosen. He'd read and read and scribbled and doodled (at least while Lillith was at school) and ever afterwards he'd considered the years spent with Evadne as his educative years. He read the contents of one shelf after the other, mainly literature with a little history, making notes and writing synopses for something of his own one day when what he'd read would have triggered something in his imagination and given rise to a viable idea.

It was all there, from Gorboduc to Ginsburg. And there it ended, abruptly in the sixties, the very year the Dean had died, as though English literature had also in that year ground to an abrupt halt, in the mother of all international writer's blocks . . .

As for their marriage, it had followed a predictable pattern. Evadne had had the veranda enclosed to make a sunporch and it was there that she waited for him every evening, with two small glasses of sherry so dry that it crimped the palate much as her lemon pudding did.

'Been working hard?' she'd ask, offering him a glass. She'd had rather nice white hands and arms, he remembered, young arms and hands (which may have been why she'd liked to play the piano), but for the rest Evadne had aged prematurely. She was wrinkled and grey at forty-five.

'How are you getting on? When do you think you'll finish?' And he would have to explain once again that creative writing was like love. It couldn't be forced. It just happened. Stole on one unawares. Like love.

Which wasn't what he had ever felt for Evadne. He'd married her house and her books. The closest he ever came to her, emotionally, was when he'd fancied himself as a sort of avatar of her late husband, slipping into his shoes quite literally, since Evadne hadn't liked to get rid of them, or of any of his clothes (it had seemed such a callous thing to do, she'd said) and since they had all fitted him perfectly, he'd slipped into the Dean's shoes, his clothes, his bed, his chair, his wife and (in Rudy's imagination at least) his daughter as well.

Perhaps there was something there after all. Something he could get down. Something about Evadne and the five years or so he'd spent in the dead Dean's shoes. Only it couldn't be too obviously autobiographical. One would have to change it, disguise it, in case she was still lurking around with her sharp eyes; in case she read it, recognised herself and sued.

So. Make her an old school friend, met by chance, and totally uncultured, as a further red herring:

'Gawd, Rudy, is that you?'

Only that was Mavis, wasn't it? Always saying 'Gawd, Rudy', no matter what he did, good or bad.

A widow anyway (that was all right, the world was full of widows) who runs a boarding-house in one of the more unsavoury parts of town. Which was where Mave came in. He'd use a composite then, of Evadne and Mavis. That would throw them both off the scent. Mavadne, his anti-heroine. Or Evadnis? Or maybe he'd have to think of something even further removed from the pair of them, to forestall litigation? Although there would be the usual declaration, about no reference intended to the living or dead, etc.

What then? He marries Mavadne, lives with her. She dies, he inherits. Which didn't happen. Unfortunately.

Because the truth was, he'd gone to jail instead, to await trial, courtesy of little Miss Lillith, the *enfante terrible*, the budding *femme fatale* . . .

He'd better not put HER in.

Not married either. Although he could just hear her, Mave again, dubiously: 'Well, it don't look too good, you know, you living here like this . . . people talk, you know.'

Because he hadn't married Mave, had he? Might have been better if he had. If he'd happened to have divorce papers . . . Might have inherited something then.

Staying with the truth (to be suitably twisted of course), winter was coming on and the alternative, cold, wet and hungry, was too terrible to contemplate. Worse, much worse than moving in with old Mave. Just for the winter, he'd told himself, to buy a little time to get himself established again, that was all.

If he really got as far as getting it all down on paper he'd have to have a name for himself as well, his alter ego, the protagonist; but then, being his alter ego, wouldn't that make him the antagonist?

He'd felt like an antagonist, the more so as the years rolled by. No more than a couple, really, but it had felt like an eternity, living with old Mave in her pink boarding-house.

Not that she hadn't been good to him. She had. She hadn't had a Lillith, though, to make those years supportable even if only in his fevered imagination.

She, the anti-heroine, then, would be warmth, shelter, food, security. Like Mave she would occasionally be strident, possessive and demanding of her pound of flesh (figuratively speaking, since the flesh in question probably wouldn't have tipped the scale at more than a few ounces). Maybe he should get a scale from somewhere, weigh it, and then add on a bit since a certain sad shrinkage had undeniably taken place? In the interests of authenticity, of course. The thought, preposterous as it was, drew him back from the edge of sleep, making him smile.

Where would he get a scale? Could he ask one of the nuns? Sister Mary Bartholomew, perhaps, since she worked in the kitchen. And what exactly would he be needing it for, she'd naturally want to know. What would he tell her?

Or should he ask Laetitia? Would she say 'olraait' without turning a hair, used to strange requests – even concerning penile atrophy – from funny old white men?

It was almost worth a try, just to see their reaction. *Sister, I need to weigh my practicals, what's left of them.* And even she might not turn a hair. After all, they washed old bodies, alive or dead, all the time, didn't they?

And that's what it had been, a dead weight most of the time, and especially at the most crucial times, with Mave. Still, who would have found it easy, making love to a boot?

Fortunately though, a token surrender, a hug or two and some sweet talk served to satisfy, although even that became an irksome requirement. It had been, in short, a costly accommodation, pricey by any standards, but with the choice between the narrow room with the single bed and tiny wardrobe for which he would have had to find the rent (impossible, at least legally) and the anti-heroine's chamber, large, comfortable, airy, with a soft double bed and other advantages, what else could he have done? So he'd subjected himself to said hugging and like ministrations and listening to her burbling on about her late husband's prodigious prowess in similar circumstances.

A late husband would have to be brought in then, an

amalgam between the Dean, the man of letters, and the Captain, the man of the sea, Mavis' dear departed.

He could be a marine biologist perhaps, which would make it possible for him, Rudy, to bring in some tidy little descriptions of the sea as well, courtesy of Lyle.

A scientist then, studying the behaviour of chokka, or whatever, in between imbibing the neat brandy which would render him senseless within three or four days of his coming ashore, after which he'd have to be sobered up with coffee and cold sponge-downs so that he could put out to sea again. Which was the way Mave had told it at any rate.

And Rudy couldn't blame him. He himself had been tempted to drink himself senseless often enough as the only way to escape Mave's smothering attentions; and his accomplishments hadn't been anything like as prodigious.

She could afford to spoil a man, she said; her little boarding-house had always thrived, and with what the insurance had brought in – a very large policy she had held on the life of the late Captain – she was prepared to spoil a man as long as that man was inclined to spoil her in return.

He saw her again, the boot as temptress, his windpipe constricting with apprehension the way it always had, anticipating imminent suffocation . . .

The trouble was, one never knew which way she was going to jump – a hug to the bosom or a broomstick to the backside (the owner of a third-rate boarding-house, widow of an alcoholic sailor to the fore at this point: Mave, the thunder-thighed old trollip rolling along on the balls of her fat little feet calling the wrath of Gawd down on all and sundry).

Evadne had been much more subtle when crossed, mercilessly pecking and puncturing his many vital self-delusions, leaving him limp and deflated as an old balloon.

It had been hard work, keeping them both sweet, especially

Mave.

Which reminded him of how hard it had been to get Mave to take him back after she'd thrown him out the first time for not paying his rent, a fateful occasion indeed and as fraught as it could possibly have been.

It had been a longish walk across the city from the park to the boarding-house and on the way he'd arranged the nicked flowers into a quite presentable little posy, reds in the middle, whites next and yellows outside, and as the posy took shape his manner became more dapper, even debonair. He had fingered his newly trimmed moustache, clipped straight across the way he liked it, and being down on his luck – the only reason any man would have for marrying or even cohabiting with a boot – he'd put his only shirt on inside out, and pulled his tie down to hide the backs of the buttons.

Having psyched himself up along the lines of 'needs must when the devil drives', he'd begun to feel quite optimistic again; so much so that when he got there to find Mavis sitting on the stoep, boot face tightly laced, he'd gone down on one knee, presented her with the posy and – to his own complete astonishment since he hadn't intended to go that far – blurted out with great feeling: 'Mavis, me darlin' marry me, why won't ye?'

The words were out and of course it was Barry Fitzgerald, Irish accent and all, only not playing the 'praist' this time. (Not that that mattered. In fact he'd had about as much right to propose as a priest, short of the proper papers as he had been.)

Well all right then, he thought. Why not? His antagonist would be Irish. Antagonistic lot, the Irish, in any case. But apart from that, nothing wrong with the Celts. He'd be Gerald Fitzbarry. Why not?

He smiled, and then, recalling the actual event again, went clammy with shock, the way he had then. Although recovery had been fairly immediate; because of course there had been nothing else for it, nothing else would have done the trick. He must have come to that conclusion as he walked (his sub-conscious must have been so sure that it was the only recourse in the circumstances, that it hadn't bothered to consult, or even inform him at a conscious level). He'd simply heard himself proposing, heard the words as though someone else were saying them.

But it was right, a good and proper thing, considering that the choice was between getting hitched to Mavis (or more accurately, and in today's parlance, shacking up with her), or jail for bilking, the Work Colony, or worst of all perhaps, living permanently with the vagrants. Even becoming a vagrant, like Claude, and especially since he had nothing like Claude's justification for ending up like that. He hadn't had a son who'd blown his head off and whose brains he'd had to collect off the floor and the walls, in order to bury him as whole as possible . . .

Of course the story kept changing in detail. Claude couldn't seem to make up his mind about the circumstances that had driven Nathan to take so drastic a step. Still, the result was pretty constant: Nathan had blown his head off, and he'd had beautiful hair, most of it ending up stuck to the bedroom wall, glued to the wallpaper like a piece of splatter-sculpture.

And naturally remembering Claude and the unfortunate Nathan made him think about Annie again, dear sweet Annie, with whom he'd been somebody, to whom he'd been somebody. Why hadn't he knelt before Annie with a nicked posy? She'd have appreciated the Irish accent. She had appreciated every-thing he did . . .

He shelved Annie, not wanting to get into that again, wanting to get on with the other saga, his fictional memoir, thinking it just might have possibilities, be different from all his other waking dreams.

So there he'd be, looking hopefully up into Mavadne's small

136

suspicious eyes, trying not to look any lower, at her raddled cheeks, or the way her bulk strained at the seams of her slacks, and spilled over the sides of her cane chair.

Poor old Gerrie Fitzbarry, more or less washed and brushed up in the public convenience in the park, having been forced to use hands and fingers in lieu of cloth and comb, with his little posy of such blooms as he could nick before he was spotted, on one knee before his bride-never-to-be, as it turned out.

It was enough to make you weep.

The question had taken some time to drop down to the appropriate level of Mavis' consciousness, or perhaps she hadn't taken him seriously, was waiting for him to jump up and laugh, indicate that he'd been joking, pulling her leg; but when it did and before he could (the thought having crossed his own mind very soon after he'd heard himself propose) she was accepting, suitably moist-eyed, scrabbling for her tissue which she'd secreted deep down in the damp pimply canyon of her cleavage.

'Rudy,' she'd whispered, dabbing at her brightly rouged cheeks. ('Gerrie', he'd have to remember.) *'Gerrie, dear boy, what would you be wanting with an old woman like me? But of course, yes. Wait till I tell . . .'*

Mavis had had several grown-up children; should Mavadne, he wondered, have just one nubile daughter in the memoir? Could he have a Lillith after all, even if only in a story, on paper? Not called Lillith, of course, but Clodagh? Solange? Or Lalage? Didn't Lalage just trip off the tongue like Lillith. Or Lolita? Could he have his satisfaction after all, even if only in his fantasies, feral top-of-thigh fetishist that he was? (*'Top of the thigh to ye,'* he could hear Gerrie Fitzbarry say . . .)

But Lillith would be on to that at once, if it, the memoir, ever saw the light of print. Better to play safe. No daughter. Not even a son.

Mavis hadn't been able to wait to tell her neighbours,

especially Nellie, who would be so jealous, she'd said, who would never believe it, because who was ever going to propose to HER again? And then she'd gone on and on about the wedding: 'Small, we'll have it small and intimate. Or do you want something grand? Do you want a hall? The kids will have to come down . . .'

By then it had been too late. The die had been cast, his fate sealed. Poor Gerrie Fitzbarry, nothing but suicide left.

He had stayed down on his knees as if imploring the gods for mercy, the posy beginning to wilt in the unseasonal heat, Mavis/Mavadne already bustling off to begin her arrangements.

'Come on Gerrie, I put that old leather suitcase of yours in the cellar, in lieu of rent, in case you came back, like I knew you would; you better get it up here before your things goes green, it's damp down there, and maybe you can look what's leaking making a mould on everything while you there, you the landlord now, Gerrie, and just bring your case up into my room, why wait? Everyone thinks you been in there with me from the first. Anyway, we're engaged now . . .'

And Gerrie Fitzbarry, ass of the ages, proverbial butt and byword, would get up, his knee aching. The new landlord.

But perhaps his subconscious had been right. Perhaps there was no price too great to pay for safety and security, for a roof over one's head . . .

'And when you've got the suitcase and checked for the leak you can bring some potatoes up as well, they're in a bag in the corner . . .'

Then again, perhaps there was.

Mavadne would go on talking (he'd need to devise some conversational quirks to fix her in the reader's mind) but Gerrie would hear no more than a rumble in the distance. She'd have gone into the pantry by then, to fetch out the goodies, the specials. There'd be a slap-up dinner that night, to celebrate their engagement; there'd be brandy and a formal announcement made to the amused, stunned boarders. Amused more than stunned, probably.

They'd all seen through the whole thing, as Mavis herself probably had. She wasn't stupid.

But they wouldn't blame him. They'd have done the same, all of them, when the chips were down, and they knew it. Marry for convenience, even gain; if they hadn't done so already. The practice was a hallowed one.

Because it had to be worth a tidy sum, the late Captain's house. (The late Dean's more so, of course, but he'd blown that one good and proper.) Best of all, it was a roof over his head, even, in a sense, his own roof, as Mave had said.

He'd help with the chores by day. Love her up at night. (Should the impish Fitzbarry manage better than he had? It was a thought. Gerrie, the carnal Celt.) And in between times (there'd be plenty of those, he hoped, since his anti-heroine would, like Mavis, spend so much of her day on the phone to her friends or spatting with her neighbours), he'd be able to go through his notebooks, see if there was something worth while stashed away and try to get back into writing. (Fitzbarry, the celebrated belletrist. And why not? Great lover, great writer; in his imagination if nowhere else.)

For Annie's sake, in a way. In her memory, in a sense, since she'd always encouraged him to get something down on paper.

'I'll have to turn up my papers,' he told Sister Mary Ambrose who had come in just then with his laundry.

'Your IDs?' she asked, peering at him over her rimless spectacles.

'Divorce papers,' he said. Now that he had again conjured up the spectre of the boot . . . (There was an idea! A horror story. He could make a horror story of his marriage to Mave/ Evadne, and without too much trouble either. *The Spectre of*

139

the Boot, or *The Haunting of Gerald Fitzbarry*.)

'Divorce papers?' Sister Mary Ambrose echoed faintly. He'd forgotten she was Catholic. And Irish.

'Well, maybe I am a widower by now,' he said. After all, it had been a long time ago, all of that, and Evadne hadn't been young, even then.

'It's all right,' he told her again, and another memory surfaced. Mave saying: 'It's all right, if you haven't got your papers, we'll have to write away for them, to the Department of the Interior, the thing is, the hall is booked and everything, we'll just have the reception in the mean time, have the pictures taken and that, then tell them we've been to the Registry Office for a private ceremony and do the legals properly later. If you've got the wedding pictures it's as good as anyway, for the kids' sake, I'm thinking of, until we can get hold of your papers and do the thing properly.'

Which meant he'd still been married to Evadne, that he had never actually married the boot; that she had no legal hold on him, even if she did try to find him again.

It was getting very complicated, the whole set-up, but he'd have all the time in the world, or at least what he had left, to unravel it and make sense of the thing; of his life, that is, if he was ever going to get it down on paper.

Perhaps there was something in all that, something that was worth getting down. But if he was going to start he needed a title. A title drew things together and focused them. A title gave thrust and a promise of substance.

Memoir was too bland, too redolent of the maunderings of genteel old ladies, soft-handed prelates and calculating politicians.

It would be about the women in his life, since his life had consisted of little else.

Or should he include the Professor of Tonsorial Artistics, *outré* as he had been; make him a Professor of something a little more prepossessing? Something to justify his bluff, audacious manner? And his mother? Should he have her, with her little blob of a nose and eyes swivelling fearfully from side to side as though she were expecting a blow?

Come to think of it – strangely, since it couldn't have been in his genes, not from the Professor's side, anyway – wasn't he himself an odd amalgam of the two, with the tension between the timid and the adventurous, the diffident and the daring? And didn't that explain it all? Wasn't it that tension that was causing all the strain, making him feel strung out, spread really thin, fraying at the edges, with large sections of his memory, his very life, stretched taut and on the point of snapping? He was stressed out, wearing out and whitening, the result of constant abuse, of merciless bleaching and battering.

That was him, Rudy, bleached and beached, no longer in the mainstream of life, hair white (dirty greyish yellow-white to be exact, like sea scum), bloated in the middle, skeletal in the extremities, full of bubbling gases and on the point of putrefaction.

Had Mavis realised what she was marrying even then (or would have been marrying, supposing he'd managed to turn up the divorce papers?).

He had never been more substantial than a slimy bit of seaweed, a rotten twist of flotsam. Beached for sure, high and dry, but even now longing for the next tide, for the surge that would lift him, free him, carry him out again . . .

But to where?

Back to Claude and the other derelicts? Back to the bins and parks and foul public conveniences? Back to dodging the law? With all that that entailed?

That had been it, the tension, antipodal as it was: the need for security AND adventure, both equally insistent, each trying to override the other, constantly pulling him apart. Three hot meals a day, or stale rolls begged from the back of the baker's? A warm soft bed (albeit, or perforce, containing either an Evadne or Mavis) or the park bench, the cardboard pallet and newspaper covers? And Zolah. That had to be said.

Those were the choices, what it had all come down to.

To be honest though, 'security' and 'adventure' put an altogether different complexion on the truth. Romanticised it.

Such choices as he had had hardly amounted to either, or anything really. He'd always been old and tired, even as a boy, and prey to the predators, the boot-faced Mavises of the world. There had even been one in school, five years older than he was, bold and buttoned-up. Called Babs. He'd had no choice but to reconcile himself to being eaten up. Eaten alive. So much for security.

And the only adventure left to him now would have to take place in his mind, in the realm of the imagination. Hopefully he could soar and wheel there, catch the currents of creative energy, reach hitherto unattained flights of fancy.

He would have to do it on paper, in little squiggles of ink on paper. That would be his life, from now on. And he would remember and relive some of the adventures of the past because it was entirely up to him. He needn't tell it all. Or even as it really was. He would embroider and enhance, take little liberties here and there so that his life could become now, in retrospect, much more adventurous than it had ever been and safe and secure at the same time. Artistic licence. The writer's prerogative. A fictonal memoir. A faction. The best of both worlds. Perhaps he could now, at the end of his days, on paper, in the imagaination, resolve the tensions, reconcile the dichotomies and truly be the ingenious, adventuring man of means he should always have been. Another of the Hemingways of the world. Or Fitzgeralds. F Scott, that is, not Barry.

It was an irresistible thought. It drew him. It could be done. It could even be published and sell?

But his optimism was short-lived. It was too late. The machinery of his life had effectively shut down and was standing idle. The lights were being turned off one by one. It was too late. He would leave no mark after all. Nothing to show that he had ever existed.

Nothing for it now but to practise a sort of mental suspension, being unable to take much pleasure in dwelling on either the past or the present and there not being much future that he could see.

He would have to exist, somehow, on the fringe of senility until he was overtaken by all that it entailed: dementia and its concomitants, mental deterioration and most demeaning of all, incontinence.

NINE

WINDING DOWN

When Rudy came in for tea, Joey was already at it, her voice shrill and accusing above the hubbub of conversation:

'Picking over Mammie's things like a box from the Salvation Army, Willem leaning out of the Studebaker with his teeth all brown from smoking.'

'Who?' Sybil asked, question marks rising.

'Bill who was christened Willem,' Joey said. 'You remember his hair was always reddish.'

'No,' Sybil said doubtfully.

'Lena wasn't much better with her thick white legs and shorts, and her lipstick running into the cracks around her mouth . . .'

Strange, Rudy thought, the way they remembered details like that but wouldn't know what they'd had for breakfast.

'Divorced now too, but maybe there was some sense in that, the way he drank and you couldn't talk to him neither. "Take the beam out of your own eye," he used to say, and "you didn't write the Bible". '

She paused to look at Sybil, hoping for some reaction, but

Sybil was staring at Nursie Thelma Rousseau who had just come in with her scissors, tweezers, files and other paraphernalia.

Sybil was getting past it, Rudy realised. If – and it was still an if – he DID decide to cultivate her, rich old childless widow that she was, he'd better get on with it. The thought gave him some satisfaction, some sense of purpose. He had a decision to make, his life wasn't completely finished . . . In fact, he should get to know old Lyle Hargood better as well, find out more about his background, who the snaky fellow was, and what he had done to his mother.

Just for now, though, there wasn't too much of a rush. He'd put it off for a bit because who knew but that having made his decisions, there wouldn't be any more to make? The sense of purpose, of having something to think about, decide on, was precious in itself, to be savoured for as long as possible. Only not too long. Not in Sybil's case, anyway.

'Well, I never said I did!' Joey said loudly.

'Did what Oumatjie?' Nursie Thelma asked.

'Write the Bible.'

'Of course not, Oumatjie, you worry too much.'

Nursie Thelma always bounced in smiling, Rudy had noticed, willing to help them with anything at all. But he'd also seen her patience wear thin as time passed and they reduced her to a physical wreck with their complaints and impossible demands and general lack of co-operation and appreciation.

What some of them needed, he thought, was to sleep out for a bit, in the damp grass, on cardboard and newspaper with the canna leaves dripping dew on their heads, eating the nondescript stuff that came out of bins (not that he'd ever sunk that low himself; he'd always managed to score something a bit better, think up some sort of scam; and with his cultivated voice, his vocabulary, he'd always managed to touch someone's heart and wallet). He'd had it good compared with some of the others.

Like the woman Zolah had introduced him to, whose face was not brown as much as purple, blotchy and discoloured by the rotgut she'd been drinking, her cheeks so puffed that the tightly stretched skin positively shone. She'd put out her hand to shake his and not wishing to offend – Zolah had proved a reliable and useful ally in so many ways – he'd submitted to the awful squelchy, sticky handshake and when he'd removed his hand it had come away full of the sour pumpkin she'd found in the bin and had been eating . . .

That was what they needed, some of them, to subsist on sour pumpkin for a while . . .

He'd never seen the woman again, but his association with Zolah had continued for a spell. Poor old Zolah (with the accent on the second syllable, which she had absolutely insisted on), the product, as she herself had said, of the violent coupling of two cultures (although of course she hadn't put it quite like that). He'd often wondered what she had meant since she had refused to elaborate: rage or passion? Rape?

Not that it mattered since Zolah didn't appear to bear any grudges. She even favoured white men and their own peripatetic fraternity in particular: Claude, Nathan's ever-grieving father, his friend Koksie Harmse (the culinary wizard, the man who could cook up something passable from the nameless; not that HE couldn't have named what he put into his jam-tin skillets, but because they had all been too afraid to ask), and his friend Floors Fatarse Froelich.

Dear old Zolah, with the accent on the 'lah'. Not that there had been anything much to it, really, at least where he was concerned. Nothing beyond a bit of banter – *risqué* as that may have been – a touch or two, a fondle here and there, a nuzzle, a tentative little poke maybe, but nothing that amounted to your actual full-blown conjoining . . .

For one thing, Zolah was usually under the weather by the time she rejoined them, she being the only one of them – in the very nature of things – who had the equipage to earn enough money to keep herself under the weather.

She was a walking small business venture, very viable financially, seeing that she had no overheads to speak of, and paid no tax.

She did a bit of running for a shebeen queen as well, Rudy had been told, but what she ran with he didn't know, liquor, drugs, guns? Probably no more than the odd bottle of brandy for those in the dimmer recesses of the city who had woken up after the bottle stores had closed.

She was also unfailingly generous, sharing with them what she had in the line of food and drink and anything else, depending on how far under the weather she was.

But even her fortunes had fluctuated. There were times when, too spaced-out to function (Rudy had often watched them pass the zolls and 'pyp' around), she was also reduced to scavenging for sustenance.

Through it all they protected her and she provided as best she could for them. No obligation. No questions asked. She even respected them, their dereliction notwithstanding, although she did inveigh against the 'Europeen' sometimes – after she'd been short-changed by a customer Rudy supposed – saying they should all have been driven into the sea three hundred years ago and it wasn't too late either, now that the political tide had turned . . .

Zolah, in fact, was more of a racist than any of them, sounding off just as shrilly against the 'keffirs' who couldn't be trusted and what was going to happen to the poor brown people now?

There was only one thing for it – and here Rudy appreciated her logic – there had to be a lot more cross-cultural coupling, violent or otherwise, until a common pigmentation, almost as great a leveller as death – had emerged to settle the issue once and for all. Which would take time, of course. And they all feared that there wouldn't be enough time; and so there was nothing else for it but to lie low amongst the cannas and pass the bottle and pipe and try to make their own contribution to the cross-cultural coupling which amounted to little more than an inept rolling around (all they were capable of at that stage) and which would hardly have given rise to a subsequent generation let alone have had an effect on its pigmentation.

Naturally none of them were really happy and least of all when they woke up the next morning in a Laocoön-like tangle amongst the wet leaves and blooms with burning eyes, bursting heads and dry mouths.

There was more to it than politics, of course, but politics was a factor, Koksie and Floors having been 'laid off' as a result of the ailing economy and had fetched up, out-at-elbows and down-at-heels, in the park with others like themselves, all of them victims of assorted adverse circumstances, not all related to the economy though, or even affirmative action, since, judging by the look of them, most had been on the road long before the New South Africa had even been thought of.

Still, any excuse was better than none and had to be milked for all it was worth. That particular line could prove lucrative too, as Rudy himself had discovered, if one approached the right sort of disgruntled character with the right sort of hard-luck story about how one had been discriminated against.

One had to have something, or someone, to blame for never having had a chance in life. He, Rudy, had his own recitation of woe, about how he and his mother had been left with a mountain of debt which his stepfather had incurred, backing also-rans at the Fairview Race Course, the result of his having listened to voices which had lied to him in his sleep.

But he could not, in all conscience, blame the new government for that. He could only blame the Professor of Tonsorial Artistics and perhaps the horses and since he, and no doubt they, had long been insensate in their graves, what difference did it make?

So there he had been, under the wet cannas at midnight, listening to the sounds of Zolah's maudlin pleading with Claude to give her a jersey which the wind had whipped off a washline and blown straight into his unsuspecting hand, something the wind had begun to do quite regularly since he had discovered Zolah's weakness for clean clothing, and who could blame her? They had had nowhere to perform their personal ablutions, let alone attend to their wardrobes.

Apart from that, liquor was expensive and there was always a ready sale for a good piece of used clothing, so if it came to a choice, there simply wasn't one. Needs must when the devil drives. And of that one thing there was no doubt, not in Rudy's guilty Catholic mind: the devil was doing the driving just then, in all their lives. They had nothing to live for, and some of them were already dying, of nephritis, and cirrhosis, had already begun to vomit and pass blood . . .

Rudy brushed the painful memories aside and turned to tap Lyle on the knee. 'Brimming with the milk of human kindness,' he said, indicating Nursie Thelma.

'Oh surely,' Lyle said mildly. 'But I was contemplating something quite other. Remembering the jasmine, you know, and the honeysuckle, heavy on the air and overpowering at night . . .'

'Quite . . .' Rudy said, thinking the man was to be envied, fixated as he was on the agreeable, on inoffensive nature with its sights, sounds and smells. Better than some of the other smells in that room full of smelly old women – except for Sybil who was wearing something really heady, expensive and French, as he'd noticed.

'You have to think good of the dead,' Joey was still whining, 'but the way they started picking over Mammie's things before she was properly cold . . .'

That was the way of it, Rudy saw. Those who might have had something interesting to say got stuck in a groove, and those who had nothing of any interest to say babbled on and on. He'd probably end up like Lyle; indeed, he'd already begun to spend most of his time with his memories.

'I wanted the Salvation Army to take it, for all they did for us during the Depression, but not them, they wanted the lot, shoulder pads and all, even that old fur cape because Lena said the bald patches wouldn't show up at night.'

'You were right,' Neville McNaughton said to Rudy. 'Schismatic lot, that's what they are.'

'Oh, the Sally Army's OK,' Rudy said. 'Lifesavers, if you really want to know.' Which was true. One could always go to them when one's straits were dire, for soup, a bath, clothes, even a bed . . .

'They did the most for us during the Depression, that's for sure,' Joey said.

'That's where Alistair went wrong,' Edna Something-or-Other broke in. 'Always spared from everything like the Depression and in the end all he could think about was girls.'

'Well, if you're a mother . . .' Nursie Thelma said. She was growing her hair, Rudy saw, and had combed it down at the sides, over her big ears. Needed another few inches or so, and she wouldn't be half bad. Young too. Not a day over seventeen?

'Whose mother?' Sybil asked, question marks quivering.

'Anybody's!' Joey snapped. 'What do you know about it, you never had any kids.'

'Alistair's mother, that's who!' Edna said. 'Or maybe Douggie's mother. I can't remember any more.' She became distressed, twisting her hanky in her lap.

'Don't upset yourself,' Nursie Thelma soothed. 'Oumatjie, calm down . . .'

'You're DOUGGIE'S mother,' Joey said. 'Alistair left you with him. DESERTED you, you said.'

'Day in, day out,' Edna moaned wringing her hanky, 'oily overalls and dirty dishes and not so much as a lousy carnation, but SHE gets a watch!'

'Kids!' Vera Myles said, shuffling furiously. 'What do you expect?'

'Who?' Sybil asked.

'His intended! Who else?' Edna said. 'Only it had got a bit beyond intentions by then. Five months if she was a day, and smiling under her eyelashes as if that was one up on ME.'

'Kids!' Vera Myles said again.

'Too fond of the limelight, that's what!' Neville said suddenly.

'Who? Her son?' Rudy asked, surprised that he should have been following the conversation, such as it was.

Neville jabbed the floor with his stick. 'Smuts! Kowtowing to the Union Jack!'

'But he's dead long ago,' Nursie Thelma said.

She must have used some sort of lacquer to hold her hair down over her ears, Rudy decided, but the strands were still too short and they were beginning to separate and stick straight up. Extraordinary, he thought. Like whiskers. Made her look more like a little pink rabbit than ever. He wanted to lean over, smooth them down. But would she mind?

'Creeping up England's bloody backside.'

'There are LADIES here. I'll thank you to remember that Mr McNaughton, if you please!'

It was the most Sybil had ever said and Rudy looked at her with renewed interest. Wealthy old widow. French perfume. Definitely childless. Nicely spoken too. Cultured. No doubt about that. Could he invite her to take a turn about the garden, he wondered? One had to start somewhere. How was she off for walking, though? She used a stick, he'd seen. How steady was she on her pins? Not that one could enquire, he didn't think . . .

'Tell you about it, if you want to know,' Neville said. 'Made a bit of a study. Always kept abreast of current affairs.'

'Smuts? Current affairs? You're way off it, Mac!' Vera said. 'Anyone feel like a game? Snap or something?'

'Alistair, Douggie,' Edna moaned, 'I can't remember any more.'

'Shut up then,' Joey said.

'No, that's not nice,' Nursie Thelma remonstrated. 'Look, it's going to rain, looks like a storm.'

'Storm?' Lyle said. 'Ah, I remember them, the storms, the air becoming heavy, and that sudden piercing chill . . . You could hear the wind coming from miles away, long before the trees began to bend . . .'

'That's where they caught him,' Edna groaned, 'behind the trees and after they locked him up we had a struggle, trying to make ends meet . . .'

'Simon left me comfortable enough, God rest his soul. I'll give him that . . .' Sybil said.

'Pity about the weather,' Rudy said to her, smiling his sweetest smile. 'Otherwise we might have taken a turn in the garden, you and I? Simon your late lamented, I take it?'

'A turn?' Sybil asked, eyebrows elevating. 'You had a turn in the garden you say? A bad turn?'

'Bad all right,' Edna said. 'Only it wasn't a garden, it was in the PARK, so they booked him and we had to live with the mice breeding in the bathroom, you could hear their little claws on the newspapers.'

'Shouldn't have hoarded them then,' Vera said. 'Mice love newspapers.'

'Promising us the earth,' Neville grumbled. 'Running after

152

us to join up. Knew where to find us THEN.'

'Who's running after you, Grandpa?' Nursie Thelma asked.

'SMUTS!'

'But isn't he dead long ago?'

Patience of a saint, Rudy decided. Nice nature. So young too. But Sybil was the one with the money. Perhaps he should try again? Choose his words more carefully? Nothing ambiguous this time. Simple straightforward invitation. Only it really did look like rain . . .

'Aye, there's the rub,' he heard himself saying out loud. Because that had always been his dilemma: rich and childish/less, or just plain child and poor? Although seventeen was hardly a child, was it? Not when sixteen was the age of consent? But consent to what? What was he capable of that would need to be consented to? That was the question.

'Destructive storms. Grand. And everything sodden afterwards, battered and dripping . . .'

'Like us,' Rudy said sadly. 'Battered and dripping.'

There wasn't too much time left, that was the trouble. He turned to Sybil again: 'When the weather clears,' he began, but she was fast asleep, her face like a dried peach covered with fine down, her pencilled eyebrows bracketing her baggy eyes. 'Some other time then . . .' he said. And from the look of the old girl, he told himself, it had better be soon . . .

Sister Mary Bartholomew came in ringing the bell to summon them to lunch. Rudy watched them trying to lever themselves up out of the chairs, floundering, puffing and panting, gasping, groaning and even gagging. It was, he thought, a sight to see.

Not that he was all that limber himself of late; still, not carrying extra weight helped. It was the lean ones, like himself and Lyle, apart from his backside, and old Vera Myles, who got to the dining-room without too much trouble.

Sybil had woken, he saw, so he proffered his hand, courtly as always, but instead of taking it she grabbed hold of his forearm, digging her nails in as she tried to hoist herself up. And even then she couldn't find her footing and with her legs sliding out in front of her, they both very nearly ended up on the floor.

There was no time to waste if he was going to cultivate her. He could see that. The old girl was clearly on the way out . . .

Reverie turned to nostalgia for times long past. Simpler times, the romantics would say, because there was a whole new world out there, taking shape just as he, Rudy, was leaving it. He'd been reading about it, the so-called digital revolution, in magazines brought in by the charitable organisations, and watching documentaries on the TV, smudgy as it was.

A high wind of change was blowing, a whole new world and way of life emerging and he would have no part in it. He was too old now, and unskilled. Technologically challenged, as they said. Or more simply, past it.

He had no more than a vague idea of the terms of reference, of the new parameters and paradigms. It was a whole new language: websites, cyberspace, multimedia, the Internet. He didn't know how to become part of it, how to point and click his way through it, how to access sites on the web which were baited with mouthwatering information, he'd gathered, a spider and fly sort of thing.

Society was changing. Everyone had caught high-tech fever. Reality was becoming virtual and intelligence artificial. Frankenstein's new monster. It was out there now. An apparently sentient, conscious thing. The almighty microchip tirelessly dispensing the accumulated knowledge of mankind. It was all there, at the fingertips of the *cognoscenti*, accessible on thousands of databases . . . Vast reservoirs of free-floating information about anything and everything, good and bad . . . No boundaries, no control. Knowledge and power.

The world was going to be run by an army of little nameless, faceless techno-fetishists, the so-called digerati, for ever ensnared in the net, locked into the images they were invoking like latter-day Fausts, manipulated by the new Mephistophelean manifestation, the cybersatan . . .

It gave one pause, it really did.

Just as well that he was winding down. It would have been too much for him. No way to catch up now. He'd fallen by the wayside of life. He'd been swept aside by the great technological tide. And so here he was, ending his life on the brink of a new beginning, a new age, a whole new cyberworld – but just how brave would it prove to be?

And with all that information at everyone's disposal, he wondered, was THE question being asked? If it was all there, and more accessible than ever before, then maybe the answer was in there somewhere as well, the answer to the age-old question. One only had to find it. Surf the net until one did, grow old doing it; but worth it, of course, if it really WAS there, in the web, buried under the mountain of accumulated information. The meaning of life, mankind's *raison d'être* . . .

But he doubted it, because as far as he could see, the web was nothing more than a noetic dumping ground, a hi-tech tip, with its contents being endlessly picked over and nibbled at by the digerati in bits and bytes . . .

Rudy sighed. He didn't have access to anything. He'd had to rely on his own puny brain and like a magpie he'd had to accumulate his own information, his bits and bites of this and that, concepts, precepts, facts and fictions. Always managed to sound more or less cognisant and on top of things too, for all that.

Although not so much of late, he had to admit. He was

winding down, no doubt about it, and the world was passing him by. Looking forward was scary. 'Futureshock' they called it, when a man lost his ability to adapt, when he realised that he was being consigned, by age or circumstance, to that portion of humanity destined to become strangers among their own kind, a sort of sub-species on the verge of extinction.

The world was changing and his tired old brain cells were no longer capable of processing the data. Better not look forward, then. Much too shocking. Like sensible old men everywhere he'd be better off looking back . . .

On further reflection, Rudy decided that he had much to be grateful for. Compared with some of the other periods of his life, the present was supportable enough. He could still hold his own in the old grey matter department, and, unlike the wheelchair brigade, he was still on the hoof.

Odd how he'd become stuck on the bovine imagery. Was it because they, in their geriatric corral, were like dumb animals just waiting for the last round-up? Or was it that incessant whine, that hum, that wheezy whispering, like the far-away lowing of a herd which knows instinctively that the abattoir would be the next and final stop?

Or had he been subconsciously reminded of the sound animals are said to make in the ritual sacrifice, when the knife explored for pain and the animal cried out *in extremis*, that being the only sound, ghastly as it was, that could summon the shades of the ancestors?

He'd have to get his mind off all that. He'd have to get busy. Get down to writing his memoir. Just the thing to spend his dying days on. In fact, practically the only thing one could spend one's dying days on.

He'd have to have some sort of outline though, to stop his thoughts from wandering in a way that would be as unintelligible to a reader as they often were to himself.

A brief chronology, then, itemising the salient features of his life and times:

The Salon – late '20s, '30s

Education and First Job – '40s

Evadne and Lillith – early '50s (with not too much to be said about the latter)

Jail, Trial and Breakdown #1 – late '50s (with not too much to be said about the former)

Psychiatric Hospital #1 – early '60s

Pypsie and Company in the Park, Gladstone in the Work Colony – '60s (with not too much to be said about any of them)

Mavis – '70s

Breakdown #2, Psychiatric Hospital #2, Annie, Aftercare Centre – '80s

The Park, Claude, Floors and Zolah – '90s (with not too much to be said about them either, especially Zolah).

And finally the Retirement Home, courtesy of the Roman Catholic Church, with its provision for a few aged indigent Catholics of which he had the fortune/misfortune to be one, and right up to the present, such as it was.

It might work. Better than nothing, anyway. He could look through his old notebooks too, mouldy as they were from having been kept in Mavis' damp cellar (he'd never been able to find that leak, not that he'd looked too hard, either).

There were some loose notes as well, stashed away in the still classy if a trifle scuffed and mouldy leather suitcase which he'd helped himself to after Evadne had shopped him to the police. Or the Child Protection Unit to be exact, although he was the one who had needed protection.

The important thing now was to see what he still had in the way of notes. One had to start with something, build on something, like sculptors used armatures, and painters photographs and sketches. Like those notes he had on the city, for instance. Historical background. He'd been meaning to use them for years. Newspaper articles, Annie had suggested. But he was too disorganised for journalism. Nothing for it now but a memoir. Dredge up the past, and quickly too, considering how little future he had left . . .

The best thing about concocting a memoir, Rudy discovered, was that one could choose which parts of one's life to be exhaustive and honest about and which to gloss over, if one mentioned them at all.

Embarrassing and demeaning episodes, like the Work Colony, for instance. Why say anything about that? Or his time on the road – or, more accurately, in the park? And yet, having thought about it now, the memories came flooding back while he stood with his finger in the dike, so to speak, trying to stem the flow.

So what of that then, the absolute worst day of his life?

He had been picnicking under a footbridge, boiling his water in a billy-can on a neat little fire fed by the pages of a telephone directory, picked up – he swore blind – and not nicked; but he'd been convicted none the less on a charge of vandalism and vagrancy and committed to the Colony along with a ragtag assortment of Claude clones; all multiple minor offenders. In other words, all simply trying to do the best they could in a hostile environment.

Talented they were too, most of them. Geniuses, some of them. Unacknowledged, of course. Misunderstood. And that, too, was the story of his life.

Rehabilitation was the primary goal. Welfare workers, social workers, psychologists, all conspired to turn them into useful, productive, independent, self-respecting, responsible members of society again.

Herculean efforts were made to rekindle the smouldering wick of the work ethic. But for the most part it had spluttered out and they had remained scavengers; like the fellow he got to know quite well, Gladstone, his bunk-mate, who had also been a writer (strange how many writers were on the road, or how many people who were on the road said they were writers). Not your actual committing-to-paper, pecking-on-typewriter-or-computer kind of writer (there having been a serious dearth of such facilities in the circles in which they had all moved); but a story-teller, a spinner of yarns, someone who really needed a scribe, an amanuensis to do the dirty work for him; or at the very least a tape recorder, an equally scarce commodity, since possession of any such equipment would have given rise to a life-and-death debate on art versus liquidity.

Gladstone had had a long eventful life and night after night he'd told his stories, meandering through them piecemeal like a latter-day Scheherazade.

They had been strange tales, part fantasy, even mostly fantasy and peculiarly whimsical; tales of Gorman and Herr Reeper, the Swiss pathologists, marooned on their little archipelago of nihilism, squeezing each other's cysts and sighing as the psychothymic pips popped, giving off little odoriferous puffs . . . Of formalin, Gladstone had said. Couldn't have been anything else.

Gorman had had the gift of hearing. The things he heard had fairly boomed in the cochlea of his being, making him long for the larger silence.

Herr Reeper, on the other hand, suffered intermittent fevers and desired nothing so much as the coolness of a cantaloupe, or a honeydew, in his mouth . . .

It was heady stuff, exhilarating, and it more than compensated for the tedium and humiliation of their daily round.

Not that they had anything to be ashamed of, he and

Gladstone had assured each other. It had been a sixties thing after all (his first time anyway) with everyone dropping out of whatever they were in and splitting like hairs, as they used to say.

'*By the time I get to Phoenix . . .*' they were all singing, without much hope of making it there, let alone to the Haight or Katmandu . . .

The authorities didn't care one way or the other. Disaffection as social protest had remained singularly misunderstood and unappreciated in the reactionary Republic, and especially amongst the unrepentant Calvinists who ran the Work Colony.

Of course Gladstone had been a little old for the long-haired hippie scene, which may have been why the courts had been unable to distinguish between honourable dropping-out and plain old vagrancy in his case.

As for himself, Rudy had never really looked the part. He'd always liked his hair trimmed and neat, influenced no doubt by the Professor of Tonsorial Artistics who'd had a pathological aversion to the neglect of things hirsute, whether on face or pate.

And so he'd been a short-haired hippie, a non-hippie hippie, an anti-hippie, doubly alienated, the ultimate outsider, a sort of poor man's Genet . . .

TEN

FADING OUT

Rudy had begun to spend more time dozing and dreaming in his chair in the lounge, perhaps because the puffy new cushions were so comfortable, so conducive to drifting off. He was recalling all sorts of things, about his association with Mavis in particular; not that he wanted to, but his power of recollection was proving as perverse as his will had always been and it took him here and there, back and forth, fetching up against Mavis, solid as ever, even in his memories.

It hadn't been a marriage, strictly speaking, although in the beginning Mavis had treated him with as much contempt as she would any husband; because, as she'd informed him, husbands were the most useless creatures on earth, a conviction that had been handed down through generations of females in her family.

He had therefore subsided into being useless soon enough, although he was not even a husband, legally speaking. She would expect nothing from him but grief and aggravation, she had informed him (although not quite as bluntly); she'd have to support him because men were lazy and she would complain about it, because what else could a poor woman do? She would be bound to annoy him no matter what she did, because men were by nature fractious.

There being nothing else for it, Rudy had sat on her stoep (from which he had had a spectacular view of the Bay), smoked and made notes, day after day, and after a while she'd revised her opinion, at least as far as he was concerned. Compared with most, he had turned out to be quite superior after all; he didn't wander around, stay away, go to the pubs, have girl-friends and come home motherless and argumentative.

Mavis was satisfied; he was better than most. He wasn't too bad, if all he was ever going to do was sit on the stoep, gaze at the sea, smoke and write.

He'd actually done a few thumbnail sketches at that time, describing the sea; a few word pictures. Not poetry, exactly, although he had made something of a game of it by deleting words here and there to see if he could produce a haiku, profound and evocative, in the manner of an Expressionist painter hurling out gobs of colour at random and hoping the result would be felicitous, or at least not too much of a mess.

But for the most part he had sat, trying to gather his thoughts, a bit of a problem – once a dreamer, always a dreamer – smoking his stogie and fingering his pen, thinking a few literary thoughts, limbering up, as it were, honing his technique by jotting down what he saw.

Not for publication, of course, but to refine his craft, sharpen his powers of observation and description, keep his eye and his hand in against that day when, miraculously, something worth while would begin to flow out of him and he'd be ready to disgorge the thing, to spew it all out, his *Bildungsroman*, or alternatively, his *roman à thèse*, teeming with the eternal verities, awash with cosmic realities . . .

Until then, he'd spent his time gazing at the sea, noting its changing moods for use later on, perhaps, as background, or even foreground. He'd caught it every morning a brilliant blue and calm like a duckpond, or grey and ugly, churned up by the wind. He'd be up bright and early, at a time when the friends and neighbours were only beginning to stir themselves, when the shop on the corner was just opening up and the meths drinkers who had been dossing down under the bushes near the North End lake came to congregate outside, brushing the grass off their clothes, shivering, hungover, hoping for a hand-out: yesterday's bread, some curled up pieces of polony, fruit just starting to develop furry spots, a few squashed tomatoes, even the bitter cold dregs out of the coffee machine.

He felt for them. Not sympathy, exactly, but fellow-feeling, empathy. That was what it was. Been there. Done that. Incredibly.

By the time the bottle store opened there'd be many more, coming to sell the empties gathered from bins all over the neighbourhood and beyond, or to collect the empty plastic containers and cardboard boxes which had been thrown out into the alleyway behind the café and which fetched quite a good price, as he knew, flattened, baled and sold by the kilo.

And every evening the scene would be played out on the stoep across the road, the impressively muscled young man would come out, bare-chested in all weathers (it had to be some kind of a macho thing), beer can in hand, to sit on the low stoep wall; and soon she'd come out as well, slim and slinky in a dress too short and too tight for her. They'd talk, kiss, caress and nuzzle, then pick, lick and lust, in full view of the entire neighbourhood.

'The love-birds' Mavis had called them contemptuously, saying it would never last; men were only loving while the honeymoon lasted and even then it was sex more than love.

'You watch,' she'd said, 'see if I'm right.'

As it turned out she was wrong. It had lasted, week in, week out, autumn, winter and spring, making Mavis even more contemptuous and suspicious of all sorts of perversions on their part, sexual and otherwise, until the young man disappeared and his old lame mother came out, leaning on her walker, to grieve at the place where he used to sit with his beer. He'd had a heart attack, sudden and totally unexpected, considering his age and the virile look of him.

The funeral with cars, family and friends came and went, and then the girl went too (she hadn't been his wife after all, and that explained everything, Mavis had said triumphantly). She was no longer welcome in her lover's mother's home. She may even have been blamed for the heart attack (over-stimulation and exertion, as Mavis had suggested).

A lopsided old bakkie arrived for her few pitiful sticks of furniture, her suitcases and boxes, and then she, like her lover, was gone, leaving the neighbourhood much the poorer, in Rudy's opinion.

But Mavis and her cronies were satisfied that justice had been done because why hadn't he married her, poor little thing? Showed how much all the displays of love and passion had meant to him. They weren't at all surprised, though. Men were like that. Selfish to the core and exploitative – and abusive, given the chance – to the nth degree. Their whole-hearted sympathies were now with the girl. (Mavis and her cronies never ceased to amaze him, the way their views chopped and changed with no regard for even the most rudimentary rules of logic.)

HE had been on the girl's side all along, of course. Lithe young thing. Healthy head of hair. Functional figure and then some. But he hadn't been able to say so, not while they were labelling her whore and slut for not being married; nor could he while they were showering her with sympathy because the rotter, her lover, hadn't married her. Mavis would only have begun the whole long whinge and whine about the time it was taking to locate his papers, so whose fault was it that SHE wasn't married?

In any case, he'd been touched by the nightly displays of love and affection. One didn't see that sort of thing too often, not practically in the street, anyway. He'd even thought that he could do something along those lines. Great lovers through the ages. Take a trot to the library and have another look at the Tristan and Isoldes, the Troilus and Cressidas, the Antony and Cleopatras; although he'd feel more at home among the Garbos and Gilberts, Bogarts and Bacalls, Lennons and Onos, even . . .

A dissertation, perhaps, sensitive and well-researched. Only whoever read dissertations? Then again, love was a good subject. Most people were interested in love . . .

'You interested in love, love?' he'd asked Mavis who had come out just then with a cup of coffee for him, handing it over with a resentful scowl in case he thought she was getting soft.

'Love?' she'd asked suspiciously. 'What's that? What're you after? You're not going to try THAT again, are you? Like last time, struggling half the night and nothing coming to anything . . .'

'Of course not,' he had said quickly. 'Quite right too.' Because what, when one came down to it, was love? Had he ever been in love?

With Mavis? Evadne? Lillith (heaven forbid), Zolah (heaven forbid even more), or Annie?

If it was as fleeting as his emotions, could it have been love? Maybe he needed to think about it. Think it through first, before trying to write about it, even now. He'd had a long life and many associations and relationships. But love?

Hadn't it been done before, though? No point in flooding the market. Or belabouring the issue. But if he did, his thesis would have to be that there was love and love. And subject to changing perceptions, like everything else these days. It had been there, not talked about much but evidenced in long marriages; the real thing, banged out on the anvil of time and experience. Now it was talked about *ad nauseam* and consummated *ad infinitum* with whoever took one's fancy, often within a few minutes of meeting. Obviously there was love, and love, as he had once explained to Annie, at quite considerable length.

There was what he'd felt for Evadne. Cupboard love. What he'd felt for Mavis. Ditto. What he'd felt for Lillith. Paternal or avuncular, he liked to think. And then there was Annie.

That had been different, and might have ended differently, if he hadn't been too old and she – an important consideration, after all – almost as destitute as he was. Blind leading the blind. There was no glamour, no sense, in starving in pairs. When it came to scavenging, reverting to one's atavistic hunting-gathering instincts, it had to be every man for himself.

Still, it was a pity, Rudy thought, remembering Annie's luxuriant hair, or luxuriating hair, since it had seemed, especially in the sunlight, to possess a life of its own.

All different. And maybe the thing was no more than physical after all. Like now, when someone had started to massage his legs while his toenails were soaking (he'd been getting terrible cramps lately and the doctor had said his circulation was poor – like everything else about me, he thought wryly – and that he could get an embolism and lose a leg, which he didn't even want to think about).

He kept his eyes closed. He really didn't want to know who it was, because it could only have been one of the large black nurses or a nun, since Nursie Thelma was off with the flu and the physiotherapist, who'd been away on a course, didn't do toenails.

It was marvellous, the sensuous feel of it: the smooth soft

fingers taking each toe in turn, gently separating it from its neighbour (strange how one's toes began to grow in towards each other protectively, or suspiciously maybe, with the passing years), massaging, stroking, soaking, stirring up, what, for heaven's sake? What was he allowing himself to get into again, at least in his fevered mind: erotic fantasies, the love-slave caressing his toes while he, the infernal lover, the dark playboy of the nether world, bided his time . . .

Before doing what? Trying it again when, as Mavis had said, nothing came to anything? Throwing himself in a fit of mad hopeless lust on a large black nurse and frightening her out of her mind, or worse still, on one of the nuns?

He sat very still, wondering if she, whoever it was who was doing his toes, would notice that something was stirring, miraculously, while he held his breath; something he had thought had given up the ghost, or its equivalant, long ago . . .?

But it didn't last long, only until he was forced to exhale and then it deflated, along with his lungs . . .

Stick to dreaming, Rudy told himself, keeping his eyes closed. Something pleasant, something that wouldn't touch him, wouldn't remind him of the mess he'd made of everything . . .

Back to the young lovers then. Of course if they had got married she'd have had the legal right to stay. The old lame woman would have been her mother-in-law. She wouldn't have had to pack her few miserable belongings into the lopsided bakkie and leave.

So why hadn't she married him? They must have been in love. Too persistent for lust. He'd never understand. He didn't know enough about love. He'd married for convenience, with the convenience applying to the circumstances not the person; the person was the price to be paid, in a sense, for the sake of acquiring the convenience.

Evadne, for instance, had had all the cons. And none of

them too vulgarly mod either. A surfeit of the sort of worldly goods that had made his mouth water: the double-storeyed house with its mellowed wood panelling and balustrades, minstrel's gallery – would you believe? – and pressed steel ceilings. And the furnishings: oriental carpets, consoles, pedestals and *armoires* . . . But best of all there was the library, and the books, in glass-fronted carved bookcases, where he'd spent so many pleasurable hours educating himself and even stringing together a word or two.

Enough of them in fact, to amount to his one and only complete work. The one place where he'd actually managed to perform the miracle of brain to page, thoughts to words, sentences, paragraphs; the thing that was like giving birth, transmitting something by much painful labour from one element to another. Electrical impulses to characters on a page, and quite as traumatic (for him at least) as the other, he imagined, of amniotic fluid to air. Only the latter was guided to birth along a canal, which made it easier, while the former had to make a sort of leap – not of faith, exactly, but something akin – through the air, from brain to pen to paper, guided by nothing, which may explain the confusion, the flurry, the reason why so much got lost in the process, spiralling off, evaporating into the ether, thoughts that would never reach page, never be captured and pinned down, or penned down. Simply lost between brain and paper, good words, sentences, paragraphs. The marvellously sublime things he'd been writing in his head all these years.

Evadne had suggested a tape-recorder when he'd tried to explain his difficulty, and why he was having to spend so many long hours in the library; but of course that didn't change anything. The gap was still there, between brain and tape, and only a fraction of deathless prose made it from inception to actual spoken word and on to the magnetic whatever-it-was.

The mechanics of speech itself somehow distracted and distorted the creative thought processes, so that he was composing WORDS not ideas, and words are common creatures, rendering everything arbitrary and banal.

Then again, maybe the ideas were no more than emotions, really, and attitudes impossible to express. In which case it was no wonder his novel had been so incomprehensible.

REAL writers, Rudy had begun to suspect, never wrote a word. It was all there in complete pristine purity in their heads; the real artists, that is, as opposed to journeymen who actually got something done. Which made the recorded world output of literature a pale sell-out, a betrayal of the miracle of creation.

What was needed — and here, of course, it would probably be too late for HIM to benefit — was a new technology whereby the writer lay and emoted in his conscious, or better still, unconscious mind, linked to strategically placed electrodes, wires and machines (still to be invented, although the little yellow men were probably getting there) which would electronically transfer the pure creative exercise from brainwaves to paper or tape, so that nothing, cramping fingers, cold toes, aching shoulders, headaches, heartaches, hunger, thirst, or any of the other trivialities of life which always managed to intrude, would debase and corrupt, irreparably, the finished product.

The novel, poem or play would simply be leeched from the writer's brain, sucked out, like an enema. It would arrive WHOOOSH! into the world, as the little electronic networks took the electrical impulses of the brain directly to a printer.

That would be the way of it, then, the writer accouchement in a sense, being delivered painlessly of the perfectly formed finished product, just like that.

A little bit of editing to be done, perhaps, but no more painful scribbling and scrabbling, of trying to catch hold of ideas just before they disappeared, crowded out by the ones following, trying to make a coherent whole of the jumble of FEELINGS which weren't WORDS and which only became words as one did violence to them and to oneself.

But as it was, and after the rejection of the *magnum opus*, Evadne had begun to fret and fuss, reprove and reproach, while he had studied, cogitated and agonised, reading and re-reading his 'notes' which amounted to little more than the odd paragraph or two, a few stray aphorisms, and a pertinent phrase here and there (pertinent at the time anyway, but soon losing their relevance and becoming as trite as everything else).

What to do? Evadne became shrill and demanding, then cold and contemptuous. He avoided her, hiding in the study where, having read just about everything else, he went on to those parts of the Encyclopaedia Britannica necessary for the completion of his comprehensive curriculum, absorbing countless tenuously related and esoteric items of knowledge. Just the sort of thing, he now thought with a little surge of hope, to add spice and variety to his subconscious which was already richly layered by heredity, environment, and the collective unconscious, all of which his neural network, connected to the electrodes and wires, would direct to be typeset (always supposing that such a machine could be invented in his lifetime, which wasn't all that unlikely, surely, considering the progress they were making with all sorts of other weird and wonderful things).

Why, he'd read that the computer's data flow could already mirror the brain, with implanted computer chips recording and saving thoughts and memories which could then be transferred directly to a machine. 'Soul catcher' chips, as they were so aptly called, plugged into the optical nerve, storing memories, smells, sights and sounds as data which could be 're-uploaded' and played back.

His own idea wasn't so far-fetched after all. Man and

machine in partnership, in a fruitful cyberunion. Although of course there was also something infernal about it, about having one's soul caught like that . . . And by a chip.

His thoughts were running away with him, as usual. Still, imagine it, being hooked up to a machine and having one's knowledge and experience instantaneously recorded, a lifetime's deposit of personalities and events, all magically transformed to become – if the very best use could be made of the new technology – the mother of all novels.

'Dreamer!' Evadne had accused. 'You're a fraud, RK. You're lazy and self-opinionated. You've done nothing. I don't think you're ever going to do anything.'

Terrible words, leaving him open-mouthed and shattered.

And then, inevitably, the comparisons with the late Dean had followed. He had been a real scholar and a gentleman, and he had produced several critical pieces, all published, and a doctoral dissertation, also published.

There hadn't been anything to say to that, but he had tried: 'If it's done, it's done. *Passé*. What's important is what hasn't been done YET. That's how fast the world is moving these days.'

Prophetic words, because who could have foreseen the technological revolution then? He'd have liked to show her – with the help of the as yet uninvented machine – what was going on in his head. Better than anything that had ever been written, by Tolstoy, Dostoevsky (was it significant that the Russians – which was not to mention Nabokov, and certainly not to Evadne – were the first that had sprung to his mind?). Although, of course, if one had been able to link THEIR brains to the machine . . .

How could he, in his delicate frame of mind, his head heavy with encyclopaedic knowledge, put up with her disdain, her strident accusations?

He couldn't, and so he'd left. Rather, he'd had the first of his fortuitous breakdowns (*après* the jail and the trial) and been taken to the hospital where he first met and forged what was to become his long, if intermittent, association with the jackbooted Chief Psychiatrist from Swakopmund, and his German nurse Hilda, short for Hildegarde or Hildebrande, he supposed, the busty battlemaiden of the electrotherapy machine. The electrodes of HER infernal contraption had had the exact opposite effect to that of the machine to revolutionise the creative procedure which he had been dreaming about. Its electro-convulsive action didn't record memories and back them up. It wiped them out, destroying data, causing the brain to crash . . .

It was so beautiful, that early morning sea, and that was the best of it, the view of the sea from the wide glassed-in veranda, and above it the sky, banded in blues and pinks with little wispy puffs of cloud like cream on the whole confection.

Rudy took up the writing pad and pen Sister Mary Benedict had given him. 'Wanting to write home then, Col Knoesen?' she had asked. A sweet woman, he thought, in spite of her squint, doing him the honour of assuming that he had a home and someone to write to. Or had it been Sister Mary Ambrose? No matter. She was also a sweet woman. A bit fixated on Ireland and the Pope, perhaps, but a sweet woman, none the less.

Maybe it was worth one last try, to bridge the gap between conception and execution before both failed him altogether. 'Wispy clouds like icing on a confection,' he murmured. 'And ships trundling in at first light trailing their shimmering wakes behind them.'

But only a Wordsworth could have done it justice. Or Lyle perhaps. Lines needed to be composed on a scene like that; it wasn't enough to string a few words together . . . And suddenly there was Annie's voice, the voice of a very young Annie, childish, almost petulant:

'But why don't YOU? Why DON'T you then?'

Or was it his own voice, his inner voice of long ago? The voice of the boy who had so persistently, perversely, disappointed everyone his whole life long, betraying their expectations and his own, ruining his chances, destroying his hopes and dreams. Of what though? Fame, fortune? Of being somebody, achieving something, having something to show for a life that had already gone into borrowed time if threescore and ten were indeed the norm?

Why not try, though, even at this late stage, as an exercise, nothing more? Pianists practised, perfecting their technique. Maybe he could do the same. Then again, fingers had to be made supple and strong when they were young, before they grew gnarled, stiff, twisted and arthritic. Was that analogous? Was it forever too late?

He must have spoken aloud because the therapist, Ahna herself, was there, right in front of him, looking at him enquiringly. (Or had he already seen her and had the sight of her, barely acknowledged consciously, given rise to his thoughts of exercise?) It was terrible, the widening gaps in his perceptions, in his reaction to the perceptions.

Or had Ahna asked him a question? And was she waiting for an answer?

'I do beg your pardon,' he said, but she had already turned away, thinking him senile or asleep, who knew? 'I was just thinking about the sea. Must have spoken aloud. Thinking about the dawn, coming up like thunder . . .'

And that took him back to the Professor of Tonsorial Artistics and the Male Voice Choir. Who knew, he might even have decided to marry his, Rudy's, mother because she had named him Rudyard Kipling, fond as he had been of *The Road to Mandalay*? Not that it mattered any more . . . Although it bore thinking about, as one of the strangest reasons anyone could ever have had for proposing marriage.

'Not quite, although it's spectacular enough, I'll give you that,' Lyle said. 'Always different, infinitely variable combinations of light and colour.'

'Infinite variety, yes, from the vastness of the universe, the cosmos, to the infinitesimal, atoms, neutrons, leptons . . .' And there it was again. Suddenly the old cerebrum had kicked in and he had remembered long-forgotten terms. For no rhyme or reason. Which only went to show how erratic his neuro-transmissions were becoming.

'Meant to do something along those lines once,' he told Lyle. 'You know, celebrate, or even just acknowledge the incredible inventiveness of nature, the Creator, if you like, the breathtaking variety of it all. Leave something worth while behind, even if only on paper.'

Rudy sighed. Maybe if he had tried, really persevered, something would have grown, developed, some plug inside would have been wiggled and waggled and worked about until it became loose and fell out and it would all have come rushing out. Who knew?

'. . . spectacular,' Lyle was saying, 'those fiery pink streaks, and those blindingly bright little rollers . . .'

'And then when it's fully up, the buildings on the foreshore thrown into relief, a one-dimensional skyline, like a movie set . . .'

'Daft, the bloody pair of you,' Neville groused.

Rudy looked down at his writing pad. There was a large blob of blue ink where he had been resting the point of his pen. Nothing more. He had written nothing. What was he trying to do, he wondered. Compile another conversation piece like the one he had shown the physiotherapist, his non-existent comments and conclusions?

And what had happened to his memoir, his story, the Colonel's story? Wasn't there something there, selective and self-serving perhaps, but still illuminating of the human condition? And without too much subterfuge, obfuscation or evasion either. Something spare. Lean and mean. No great grey fog of vaporous phrases. No confections. No time for that now. Just the facts (some of them anyway), sincerely and honestly and for once in his sorry life?

'How come we're the only gents in this section?' Rudy asked. 'You and me and Lyle?'

'The old girls outlive us, don't you know?' Neville said. 'They see us under every time. So who's the weaker sex I'd like to know.'

Most of them were still puffing and panting from the physio session, except for Joey who refused to do anything physical, saying that she had suffered enough in her time and mostly at the hands of her daughter-in-law who was a nasty piece of work and no mistake.

'Pleading with her, standing in the street knocking at a door that had a piece of cardboard where the glass should've been and a piece of gum stuck in the hole where the bell should've been . . .'

'Ahna,' Rudy said to the physiotherapist, who was busy packing up, 'let me give you a hand, my dear . . .' but to his surprise his body didn't respond to the command to get up smartly, to relieve her of her burden of tape-recorder and manual of special exercises for the moderately disabled. Somehow his legs lacked the leverage, the muscle-power, or whatever it was that he needed; his arms were too weak to lift his body up from the chair. Only his mouth responded with a sweet smile as he heaved and pushed and finally struggled upright.

'Take it easy now Colonel Knoesen,' she said. 'Just look how you're shaking. I can manage . . .' and by the time he had begun to lumber towards her she was already closing the door, her burden securely held in the crook of one arm, steadied under her chin.

There was nothing for it but to sink back into his chair. At least he could still sink, he thought, and especially now that the good congregation of St Barnabas had provided them with really fat, springy cushions. Best face it: it was the sedentary life from now on, the gentle decline, taking it easy, as Ahna had said, conserving one's energies, making the most of what was left for as long as one could . . .

'Ten o'clock in the morning . . .' Joey said loudly.

'In your dreams,' Vera Myles said. 'It's nearly lunchtime.'

'. . . and she's still in her dressing-gown and I had to push in, didn't ask me to sit down, oh no, just went on stirring something on the Primus and flicking her ash into the empty curry tin.'

Nursie Thelma came in with some old magazines. 'And how are we all today?' she sang out.

'We've had it, if you really want to know,' Rudy said gloomily. 'The sands of time, all that . . . We've had the best of it, I fear . . .'

'People always complaining,' Neville said, 'but where did it all start?'

'You mean, life?' Rudy asked, surprised. 'Where did we all start?'

'South African Party, United Party, but you want to go right back, to what the three Boer generals were trying to do . . .'

'Well . . .' Rudy began but Joey interrupted:

'Never even offered me a cup of tea. I had to take a bus and walk, uphill all the way, and there she's standing with the baby on her hip . . .'

'I don't know what you mean exactly . . .?'

'BABY!' Joey said savagely. 'Don't you know what a . . .'

'About the Boer generals!' Rudy snapped. 'I'm talking to Neville! Trying to.'

'Before our time,' Neville said, banging his stick, 'but that's where it all started.'

'Wanted to choke her,' Joey said. 'The little minx . . .'

'Manx,' Sybil said. 'MANX. Had one myself. Tisket. *Tisket, tasket,*' she began to sing, '*I've lost my little* . . . SIMON!' she called suddenly, making everyone jump. 'I've lost my little . . .! SIMONNNN . . .!'

'It's all right, Grannie,' Nursie Thelma soothed. 'Don't worry. It's just her little cat.'

'Look what she made me do,' Vera Myles complained, 'cards all over the place . . .'

'SIMON!' Sybil called again.

'Your dear departed?' Rudy enquired sympathetically, but she stared blankly at him, not even raising her eyebrows.

She was out of it, he decided reluctantly. Rich and childless as she was, it was too late. The woman was right out of it . . . But then, so was he. Practically.

'That's when the seeds were sown,' Neville said.

'Seeds,' Lyle echoed. 'Reminds me of that snaky fellow with his catalogues, slithering behind my back to Mother.'

'This thing with your mother and the snake. Do you realise how Oedipal it is?' Rudy asked.

'Cold reptilian chap with his soft sibilant . . .'

'Yes?' Sybil enquired, question marks rising.

'Not you, dear. He said sibiLANT,' Rudy said. 'You know, hisss . . . snaky . . .'

'Snake in the grass all right. What did he ever do about NATION-BUILDING?'

'It frets me,' Joey whined, 'because she's going to be the one picking through my things.'

'All the promises, oh aye,' Neville said. 'But what did we get? Boils!'

'Here,' Rudy said to Nurse Thelma, 'how old are you, my girl?'

'Twenty-one, but I wouldn't tell everybody.'

'You look younger. Seventeen. Seventeen, I thought, if she's a day.'

'That's because you're so old Grandad, I mean, Colonel.'

Grandad, Rudy thought. All right then, what about a grandfatherly pat on the arm, squeeze of the knee, tweak of a soft pink ear? What about that, then?

But she was well beyond his reach. He'd have to heave himself up to give her a tweak or a pat, and he'd never make it. He could call her over, of course . . . Should he call her over . . .?

It was too late. He'd lived his life, such as it was. And at least he'd spent part of it with Annie. The best part. They had both been so much better in the Aftercare Centre, when the pendulum had come to rest more or less in the middle at last. She'd responded very well to treatment, her moods had stabilised; but it had saddened him to hear the prognosis: lifelong maintenance therapy, she'd told him, or she'd be in and out of institutions for the rest of her life.

Not that he hadn't been in and out of institutions of one sort or another himself: the psychiatric hospital, the Aftercare Centre, and now the old-age home . . . not to mention the colony and the chooky, the joint, the hard place, or whatever they called it these days. Sun City.

Not too much to choose between any of them either, when one came right down to it, dingy and cheerless as they all were. But the overpowering sense of drabness, hadn't that been an institutional thing, the result of unalleviated boredom, of the tediousness of their existence, their quality of life, between the four walls of the wards, the dining-rooms and the lounge? Unspeakably dreary days, congregating in the small courtyard or on the stoep to catch a few rays of the sun. And even the sun had seemed weak and grudging in its warmth in the 'new place' as he and Annie had called the Centre.

At least it had been quiet there, unlike the 'old place'. Or the present place, the Home, where the noise was incessant, that low-pitched hum punctuated by shrieks and begging and pleading for who knew what. The same sort of noise as in the 'old place', which wasn't surprising since the inmates were all much the same: psychogeriatrics and psychotics . . .

The quiet ones were the same in both places too, those who were mentally impaired with age as they gradually slid into oblivion, and the severely disturbed as they were turned into zombies with drugs, the 'chemical strait-jacket' and the psychotropic cocktail.

Rudy remembered the effects, the inertia, the brief stabs of panic as one tried to regain control of one's will, one's thoughts, or at the very least, of one's drooling; when the mental muscles, artificially relaxed like the labial, just wouldn't respond and all one could do was dribble.

Annie had been far worse. Compared with her he'd been depressed within the mild-to-mellow range, out-of-focus, a bit smudgy intellectually, dipping down to disorientation occasionally, a bit incoherent, but not much more than *Weltschmerz*, not really.

Annie, now. There was a full-blown bipolar affective blow-out, one for the books: disordered sleep, total inability to concentrate, hypochondriacal delusions, and a low-spiritedness that had bottomed out deep in the slough of despair; and it was that that he remembered most clearly: the lovely girl's morbid, self-deprecating tendencies.

He'd tried to console her but she had been impervious . . .

And then there was the other side of the clinical picture, when her dark mood lifted, rising rapidly towards uninhibited hilarity, when she became hyperactive, prolix in the extreme, and completely irresponsible; a hypomania resulting from nothing more than brainwaves gone totally and independently berserk.

At such times there had been that heart-rending panic and confusion in her eyes, that bewilderment, as if she were baffled by what was going on inside her own head, by her actions and her words, as though she'd been taken over by another, wild crazy thing, used and abused like a ragdoll, hyped-up and tossed about in a strange euphoria demonic in its intensity . . .

Still, they'd come out of it, he and Annie, caring for and supporting each other. In fact, Annie really had come out, he thought, remembering that day on the Hill when she'd come looking for him, when he'd not been able to respond in any way, covered with embarrassment and shame as he had been, leaving Claude to speak for him. Not that there had been anything to say, of course. Annie had changed. There was something totally different about her, her whole appearance and bearing. And he hadn't known how to respond to that.

She'd broken out, escaped; he could see that. But how?

And why had his life continued on its downward spiral? Had, in fact, taken a severe dip, seeing that he'd had to go on the lam soon after and at a time when he was way too old to even pretend to being a free spirit, a social protester or a rebel with or without a cause. Too old to deceive and exonerate himself with THAT little myth. It may have been a matter of his own sovereign choice, but the lack of viable alternatives had limited him somewhat. The choice, after all, had been between going to ground, and going to jail. Or community service for bilking, with the latter the worst of all, perhaps.

The memories were becoming so disturbing, so fraught with significance, for all his somewhat diminished perceptions, that Rudy decided to go and sit outside, so as not to be disturbed by Lyle's effusions or Neville's explosions, or the gibberish that the pickled bums were always mouthing . . .

He sat down on the bench near Sister Mary Bartholomew's kitchen garden to ponder and give consideration where it was so clearly due:

Annie had somehow been released, and it had had nothing to do with her being discharged from the Aftercare Centre. He'd seen that clearly, and maybe that was why he'd been so dumbstruck, sitting like a fool, looking out to sea, unable to say a word. She was a stranger, that was why. She'd changed completely. Her eyes were bright, there was a bloom on her skin. On her life. He could see that.

She had looked straight at him and said something that he'd only half understood:

'That way leads to the abyss,' she'd said.

Was she being philosophical? Religious? Was she trying to tell him that her own course was fully charted – to pursue their old shipwreck metaphor – that she was safe at last and sailing towards a sheltered haven, while he was still tacking from one jolting shipwreck to another; or no longer even in the boat, but struggling now to keep his head above water, hanging for dear life on to whatever flotsam happened to come bobbing by?

In a way it had sounded like the sort of proposition he'd rejected years before, preferring to remain aloof from any sort of elitism, any suggestion that there was only one way, with the alternative being the abyss, the outer darkness. Although at the back of his mind there had always been the worrying suspicion that that was a cop-out of sorts. Because why SHOULDN'T there be only one way? Why couldn't the choice be that simple? THE way or no way?

For his own part he had preferred the abstractions of the demythologising priests, which spoke to his own sterile intellectualising.

Still, after all the years, after a long lifetime, what conclusion had he come to? What reason for being? And now that he was on the very brink of eternity, what hope after death?

He'd found it difficult to believe that the 'way' she had found would have addressed any of his needs, and certainly not the most immediate, which had been to avoid the law at all costs, to which end he had even had to shave off his beloved moustache.

In any case, nothing was for nothing. He'd learned that. One of the prime lessons of his life, actually, beginning with Evadne and ending with Mavis; the former insisting on creative activity as the price for taking him into her home and bed, and the latter insisting on his just BEING in her bed, at a time of his life when the years had taken their toll or, possibly, when disinclination had become disability. Disrepair from disuse. The fact was, she had simply been too old, too flabby, too sweaty, too hairy.

Whatever had possessed him (not that he didn't know), he who had always had a predilection for the pubescent, the smooth and the tender? And so, when he hadn't come up to scratch (how she'd rubbed that in, with her crude references to little men and their big cigars) she'd thrown him out, reminding him that she was his landlady, and not his wife, since he hadn't ever managed to get hold of the probably non-existent divorce papers (which he for one didn't regret).

She'd simply been too post-menopausal. That was it. With hair where there shouldn't have been and bald patches where there should have been.

Ah well, he had nothing left now. Not even the cigar. And

that was the crux of it, really. Nothing left.

So what would it cost, accepting help in a time of need, supernatural help, the sort Annie was obviously meaning? She hadn't actually SAID so, if his memory served him (and he seemed to be on some sort of roll at the moment, with all the things he had been dredging up), but that was what she had meant. That something supernatural had happened to her.

And he believed it because she'd looked so different that last day on the Hill. She looked normal, but in a heightened sort of way; she looked happy – concerned for him, of course – but still happy, joyful, with a deep full joy that one could sense despite the overlay of concern, real concern, real loving concern. She was obviously on the way, as she'd said. She didn't look as if she needed therapy any more, maintenance or otherwise. And she'd urged him to get into the way as well because the way he was on led to the abyss.

But again, at what cost? Acceptance of supernatural help meant dependence and obligation.

The thought made Rudy smile. What did he have in mind? A sort of celestial Mavis, heaving and panting and sweating, great rolls of lard quivering, demanding his services? Not in a physical way, of course, not to be serviced; but service, none the less. Deeds and words, love and serve. Thought, word and deed. That much he knew.

ELEVEN

GOING UNDER

What Joey had been saying may have influenced him after all. Perhaps one did need to decide on the disposal of one's effects. But what would the Sally Army make of his? The notebooks, for instance, Debenham's portrait and the other bits and pieces in the battered leather suitcase?

Annie might be intrigued, though. And he owed her something, the way he'd ignored her that day on the Hill. He needed to explain himself, or try to. He'd write her a letter he decided, and leave it in the suitcase together with his last will and testament: everything to Annie, Miss Anna Owen Welles, c/o The Good Samaritan Aftercare Centre, Hill Street, Port Elizabeth.

Hopefully they'd have a forwarding address and pass it on to her.

Having made up his mind, Rudy got the writing pad Sister Mary Ambrose had given him. No time like the present after all, especially since there couldn't be too much of it left. He'd start with a quotation, to prime himself, get the old juices flowing. Annie had liked quotations as much as he had, especially irrelevant ones.

My dear Annie, he wrote. *'Love is strong as death.' Not as pointless as it could have been perhaps, but it comes from my heart. I am, you see, on the point of 'a sleep and a forgetting', suffering quite violent intimations of, not immortality, but the other, and unlike your own dear self, lacking 'the faith that looks through death . . .'*

I am leaving you all my worldly goods. Please see that the Salvation Army gets the cuff-links, the studs and my underpants. And tell them that they may NOT be used for dusters. This is vital. I cannot explain here.

My oeuvre, *such as it is, may interest you more although you will see at once that I never did resolve the dilemma of whether or not to concern myself exclusively with form and style considering the proportions the problem of mere content always assumed.*

You will see also, when you come to read the black notebooks and other assorted pieces, that I was thinking in autobiographical terms, a sort of poor man's 'Golden Notebook'. Alternatively, something à la 'à la Recherche du Temps Perdu', although heaven knows I could never aspire to anything like Proust's syntactical elegance. Or did his measured, monotonous style, his power of total recall, or what he was pleased to call (or alternatively, what it pleased him to call?) his 'sort of fecundity of mind' only give an illusion of the sublime?

I have often wondered.

The trouble is that there was nothing in my experience to inspire me to poesy in the way that lime-flower tea and the scallop-shelled pastry of a little madeleine might, even supposing I had the Proustian gift of being able to conceive of a biscuit in terms of 'severe religious folds'.

I was therefore constrained to remain on my own literary

level, aiming at no more than an unassuming but I trust appealing blend of fact and fantasy, a kind of Swann-through-the-looking-glass. Always hoping, of course, that my own fecundity of mind would rise to the challenge. You will, I am sure, pick up on all this.

I must confess then, to the creation of things past here and there and woven into those actually remembered, in the hope that they would introduce an element so tantalising as to make up for the coherence — spurious though that may be — which would otherwise be lost. (Or, make up for the loss of that coherence, even if spurious, which it might otherwise have had?)

Forgive me. The possible permutations of everything I write always intrigue me. I will need to control myself, to consider each sentence as irrevocable as a roll of dice, resisting the impulse to go back, give a few more shakes and fling them down again in order to contemplate the new pattern the words have made.

I was, I suppose, trying to untangle the hopelessly snarled-up skein of my life, to find out where it all began. Maybe I should have taken an existential stance instead and become committed to something, embraced something. (Or someone? Would that do? But what? Or whom?)

Then again, it might have been better to have foregone commitments and stances even at the risk of losing some substance . . .? You may decide for yourself.

If the notes are worth editing, collecting, selecting or collating, would calling the resultant anamnesis 'Swann Song' be too evocative? Or provocative?

Unless of course you decide that it is all too immaterial and inconclusive to be a memoir, or even an apologia . . .

But remember that the 'Literary Companion' said of Lessing's Notebook that it was 'interesting, but its form . . . awkward, consisting of incidents and extracts from notebooks, some diaries, some stories'. I have always liked that. The expedience of it. What does one put down after all, if all one has to offer are incidents, extracts and stories?

And that, dear Annie, is what you will find in my own notebooks. Minus the great chunks vaporised by the ECTs and without which the what? memoir? might conceivably lose its continuity (or which might conceivably cause it, the memoir? to lose its continuity?). You may fill in the gaps with anything that you consider consequential.

In short, I never did manage to get all the 'temps perdu' down, mainly because most of the 'temps' were so completely 'perdu'. As for the rest, it never quite clicked, focused, or became contiguous to anything, I don't think.

Still, do the best you can, dear Annie, memoir, biography, whatever.

You may not like the title 'Swann Song' either. You may think the line between the richly allusive (Proust, Carroll, Tchaikovsky et al) and the merely eclectic just a little too thin?

I would like the lovely lady so beautifully captured by Debenham to go on the dust cover, if it gets as far as that, and mainly because I haven't the vaguest idea who she is. If you could include a poem or two as well from the least foxed of the verses, especially the darkling woodland one, I would be much obliged.

You may keep the framed accolade if you like. If not, the Salvation Army might want it.

And be kind, dear Annie, as you come to read. You will, in a sense, be looking into my soul.

That was it, all he had to say. He'd have to find a suitable way of ending the letter, some way of letting Annie know how much she'd meant to him. But perhaps he already had, with the quote from the Canticle? He hoped it wasn't too obscure. Because the devil of it was, he more than half meant it, he really did.

Rudy knew something was failing or had failed long before they moved him to the frail care section. It was more than mere weakness, aching muscles and the strange spasms. Intermittent fever, the doctor had said; lungs, and 'be careful of the heart'.

He'd been amused to see Sister Mary Benedict compressing her thin lips and nodding, wondering how she thought she was going to do that, take care of his heart.

'Breathing's out of kilter,' he'd told the others before they moved him.

'Not the only thing either,' Neville had agreed matter of factly.

And of course that was the way to respond. Death was simply a fact of life, wasn't it? The way of all flesh.

How melancholy, Rudy thought. He hadn't found the meaning of life yet – too late for that in any case – and now, at the end of his allotted span and then some, would he discover the meaning of death? Did the one justify, or make the other more significant?

His allotted span and then some . . . a sort of bonus, since it certainly hadn't been by reason of strength, physical or moral.

He missed his own little room and his nameplate. In the frail care ward he was part of an anonymous lot, a Boschian bunch, vague and uncomprehending, their white, wispy heads sunk into their pyjama collars, staring out with milky eyes, black hairs growing out of their noses and ears, suffering from every ailment known to man, their arms, hands, legs and feet ulcerated and covered in crusted bandages.

The noise was terrible, the sniffing, the snorting, the hawking, coughing, moaning and groaning; but worst of all was the whispering, that sepulchral wheezy whispering, that incessant, pervasive hum that vibrated through the place as though everyone was sighing softly; the sort of sound one heard in horror movies just before Lugosi or Karloff stumbled in. It was mood stuff, menacing monster stuff, inducing a shuddering dread.

He wouldn't be able to take it, not for long; too appalling by half, it was . . . Only the doors of the ward were electronically controlled, there were angled mirrors everywhere; it would be impossible to escape. They were prisoners, all of them, not least of their superannuated bodies. No wonder they were all groaning. A day or two and he'd be at it as well. He began to hum under his breath, getting just the right note, the right sort of undulating wave of sound, soft, louder, soft again: 'memeaheeaheemee . . .'

And would that be it, he wondered, until he gave up the ghost, a ghost being what he practically was already? Or would be very shortly if he stayed there, of that he was certain. The 'dump' they called it, because they'd all been dumped there, human refuse, no further use for any of them, their organs shot, useless for transplants, nothing else worth recycling. Except as compost:

Then worms'll come an' ate thee oop
On Ilkley moor baht 'at . . .

They brought nothing over but their toiletries, their night-clothes and those few treasures which wouldn't take up too much space: photographs, letters, reminders that they had belonged somewhere, to somebody, once.

He could have brought the Debenham portrait but he preferred to keep it safe in the nicked suitcase, where Annie would find it.

Fear of dying gripped him. There must have been a reason for the relentless scrolling-down of his life, over the last few months, together with the memories of past deceptions and sodden sinfulness in the company of people like Claude and Zolah. Not to mention Lillith. Although he hadn't done anything there. Not really, not much.

What was it about staring eternity in the face that could reduce the bravest of men – and he'd always considered himself as intrepid as any – to cold sweating fear?

He forced himself to consider the question. Fear of the unknown? Primarily. Which led the ancients to mythologise it: Styx, Cybele and the dog. What was the dog's name? Not Rex, or Rover, he didn't think. And the ferry, the fearsome ferry, sailing smoothly on the oily, inky waters, making no sound, not even when the ferryman dipped his black oars in . . .

Was it all that?

Or not the fear of dying so much as the fear of dying alone? Unless one counted the priest who was bound to come in to administer extreme unction. Which made him wonder whether he could ask that he be sprinkled with the holy water BEFORE he breathed his last, because who knew what miraculous effect the water might yet have, even at that late stage?

Then again, would he want to be resuscitated? Even now, before he'd reached the actual deathbed stage, life was no longer what it had been. Not too much fun any more. His eyes weren't what they had been either. He struggled to breathe, with his chest wheezing away like an old kettle on the boil ('We'll have to be watching you for pneumonia, Colonel Knoesen'); his limbs cold as ice and prickly with pins and needles ('We'll have to be looking out for thrombosis, won't we, Colonel Knoesen?'). And even his heart, the one organ he'd always considered stout, and not only metaphorically, had been pretty erratic of late (too late to watch out for anything there, he'd gathered, since the Sisters Mary had all begun to enquire gravely: 'When did you make your last confession, Colonel Knoesen?').

So there it was. The dichotomy. The paradox. Both longing for (in a way) and fearing (very definitely) one's last call. Uncomfortable in either world, so to speak, having made peace with neither. Life hardly worth living. But not yet ready for death, not by a long chalk.

For one thing, he was sure he'd be alone. The nuns and the nurses would look in but they wouldn't have time to stay. They'd leave him to get on with it, die and get it over with, so that the priest could sprinkle, the nurses could wash, the undertaker could lay out or parcel up or whatever they did (he'd never really wanted to find out); but at least, since the cause of death would be considered 'natural', he wouldn't be subjected to an autopsy, there would be no need for anyone to lay his bones bare with a bistoury . . .

Still, one needed someone at the last stage of life; a relative, or at least a close friend. Too late for either, in his case. Last of his line, and too old now to make and really cement a friendship, or a marriage of the sort that only death could part.

He should have thought of it before. If he had been able to keep his hands off Lillith, Evadne would have done him the deathbed honours (she might well have lived to do it, judging by the ages of most of the old doxies in the Home). Alternatively he should have stuck it out with Mave. Only she'd been bound to precede him, judging by her bulk, fluttery heart and breathlessness which had almost amounted to a death-rattle.

No. If he'd stuck it out with Mave, he'd probably have had to do HER the honours long ago, held her hand, assured her that she was going to a good place, that she hadn't led too bad a life; that she'd done some, hopefully enough, good things to ensure a reprieve from too dire a punishment.

But just how convincing would he have been able to be? How convincing could anyone be, supposing someone did come and try to ease HIS final passage?

No point in even considering Annie. Too late for that. Still, he drew some measure of comfort from the thought that Annie would be taking care of his papers, his *oeuvre*. She would one day, in a sense, be holding a very vital part of him in her hands. It was as much as he could hope for and more than he deserved . . .

Annie had got it together, somehow. No doubt about that. She'd moved on. Might even have married by now. Why not, after all? He only hoped her husband appreciated her.

Thinking about Annie made him more and more despondent. What had possessed him to make such a hash of everything, fetching up in a Home full of old scrubbers with their smeared lipstick, spotted crimplene, and gnarled toes protruding through the holes in their felt slippers?

He didn't know which were worse, those who still took the trouble to smear some lipstick on, even if it made them look like waxwork hags, or those who sat hour after hour staring dully at nothing, who had given up on their appearance, wearing the same old clothes day in and day out until the nurses forced them to change.

Not that he'd been doing much more than staring dully himself lately.

And he wasn't even allowed to ease his passage into the unknown with a bit of tobacco, not that he had the wherewithal to acquire a cigar or even a cigarette. Begging had been useless. ('With your lungs, Colonel Knoesen? And your heart? Heaven forbid!') Amen, Rudy agreed, although he seriously doubted that heaven still cared what he did.

But he was an artist, he told himself (without really believing himself any more) and an artist needed no one, except as a sounding-board; practically anyone would do, which was the point he had tried to make in his abortive novel. Anyone could have played Dorothy to his Wordsworth, Hendrickje to his Rembrandt. It didn't have to be Annie . . .

It was all very depressing, but it could have been worse. At least he was well looked after and everyone was very kind. Better than dying under a bush, a beatnik to the bitter end, with dogs sniffing around preparatory to lifting their legs.

Rudy remembered the horror stories they used to swap, he and the others, of corpses among the cannas half-eaten by dogs and rats, which was far worse than the worst goings-on in the frail-care sections of some Homes, and there were bad ones, by all accounts. They'd all heard stories about pinchings, slappings, fallings – with brittle old bones broken, undetected and unset for ages – of urine-soaked sheets left unchanged, and of course, the gross abuse of tranquillisers and sleeping pills.

Not that one believed everything one heard. But they moaned about anything and everything, believed anything, especially shocking things. Still, the reports in magazines and newspapers were consistent and persistent enough to give one pause. He wouldn't have minded the pills, he thought. Used to those. Even the pinching and slapping, as long as he could retaliate (thinking of Nursie Thelma, incorrigible old roué that he was). But he hated the smell of urine, especially stale urine. ('We'll have to be doing something, Colonel Knoesen, won't we now, if you're losing control of your bladder?')

Not that one could blame the nurses for everything either. They had to be sorely tried, God knew, by those who insisted on wandering off, who themselves slapped, swore and reviled with the best of them, who screeched for hours on end, day and night, or wept endlessly, loudly, like small children; who threw tantrums whenever they saw soap and water, refused bedpans and then wet the bed, the floor. Some of the old men used the wash-basins, he'd heard, the showers, the bath, the flower-pots, their water jugs, anything . . .

Turning them into duffies with sleeping pills and tranquillisers became a viable option, in those circumstances.

He didn't want to end up like that. Perhaps death would be preferable after all. A good, clean, quick passing, please, he prayed to whoever might be up there, listening. Although it was a cheek, really, asking for favours in death when he'd been pretty careless of all things religious in life. ('Say one for me,' he used to call gaily as Evadne and Lillith were leaving for the Mass.)

Still, there couldn't be anything worse than facing eternity with all one's faculties intact, one's eyes wide open. Failing the good, clean, quick dispatching, it would be better to be so senile and demented and totally out of it that one didn't even realise one was dying.

Many of them there in the frail-care wards were no longer aware of anything. They simply lay in their beds, refused food and water, slowly starved and dehydrated, and gently drifted off into the unknown, feeling nothing.

Laetitia had assured him of that as soon as she'd finished sneezing: 'Olraait, they doan feel NOTHING, hokaaay?'

Nothing. *To die, to sleep; To sleep: perchance to dream . . .* And just there was the rub, exactly. The bard had put his finger on it, for in that sleep of death, who knew what dire dreams would come? In the abyss, the deep, did one dream of eternal fire? Or did the fire consume one's dreams, all that one remembered of life. Was that death?

Death consigned one to Hades. Ferried across the Styx by the surly Charon, passage paid for with the coin laid in dead mouths under dead tongues by caring relatives. And after that

194

one had to propitiate the devil-dog Cerberus. (Ah! Rudy knew the name would come back to him!) How did one propitiate him, though? He didn't remember; if he had ever known.

What he did remember was that the Greeks hadn't even been able to decide on exactly how many heads the hound of hell had: three, or fifty? Could one take any of it seriously then? The other rivers for instance, of woe, flames and wailing which had to be crossed before one could finally drink at Lethe, the river of forgetfulness?

If the ancient Greeks had got it even half-way right (a moot point, admittedly), dying was as fraught as living had ever been, at least until one got to Lethe and oblivion . . .

All the more reason then, he decided, to partake gratefully of whatever drugs and sleeping potions they were dishing out. Pre-empt fate, as it were, beat the gods at their own game. Lethe was Lethe, however and whenever one came by it.

Not that he took all that seriously, of course, but the grain of truth principle had to be respected. Because one never knew.

Then again, perhaps one COULD have known if one had only taken the trouble? Studied the Hebrews instead of the Greeks? Or even his own lot, the Romans?

Too late, Rudy thought. But perhaps it would be all right just to take it easy, to rest for a while . . . He was becoming so uncommonly tired . . .

He wasn't surprised to see that they'd sent a priest in, a stranger – although why should he have been expecting Father McGillivray? He wasn't in the Centre any longer, he was in the Home where Father Lacey did the honours, Lacey with his pale puffy face, his clerical collar barely visible under the folds of his double chin.

Rudy didn't move his head, the effort was simply too much for him. He looked at Father Lacey sideways, through watery eyes. His lower lids had begun to sag, collapsing inwards so that the lashes swept across his eyeballs like tiny wipers, scratching and burning. ('Trichiasis, Colonel Knoesen, that's what it is.')

Father Lacey looked as if he'd had a bad night as well, Rudy thought. His eyes were shot with tiny veins and an angry-looking eczema had spread across his cheeks and chin. Barber's rash, perhaps, rare in this day and age. What had the man been up to?

'And how are you?' Father Lacey asked, bluff, reassuring. Strangely, he hadn't called him 'my son'. Perhaps they didn't do that any more?

'Tired,' Rudy said. 'Bone tired. Not quite so feverish, but it comes and it goes.'

'Is there anything you'd like to tell me?' Father Lacey asked, more gravely now, and again the unspoken 'my son' hung on the air. This was an official visit, Rudy understood. Spiritual business, seeing that he was either *in extremis* or well on the way to getting there. 'You'll be needing to unburden yourself?'

Rudy made an effort. After all, it was nice of the man to come, especially since he, Rudy, hadn't exactly been a faithful son of the church. In fact, baiting and challenging Father McGillivray at the Aftercare Centre had been the closest he'd come to matters pertaining to the faith in a very long while. But what was there to say now?

'I've buried my burdens, Father,' Rudy told him. 'Exhumation at this stage might be hazardous. Best not to disturb them, the shards and artefacts of my life, the phantoms, the shades . . .'

'Exorcism . . .?' Father Lacey enquired doubtfully. He wasn't prepared for that, Rudy saw; not that that was what he had meant.

'Too late in any case,' Rudy said wearily.

'Never,' Father Lacey leaned forward, adopting a suitably solemn tone. 'It is never too late . . .' and then it came: 'my son. You will want to make your confession . . .'

'Too late,' Rudy said as decisively as he could. 'I don't rightly remember any more, apart from odd, irrelevant things. My memories have been shredded by Hilda's infernal machine, scattered this way and that, like tickertape in a high wind . . .'

'You'll be needing to unburden yourself,' the priest said again. Rudy had the impression that that, and nothing else, was the purpose of the visit and the sooner it was achieved, the sooner the priest could get back to doing whatever he would otherwise have been doing. He went through the litany quickly: when was his last confession? When did he last attend Mass?

Rudy shrugged. He couldn't remember. Had he ever? 'I think I may have misunderstood . . .'

'We've all misunderstood,' the priest conceded.

'What day is it?'

'Tuesday.'

'Tuesday! What happened to Monday? And Sunday? I can't afford to lose any time . . .'

Father Lacey had begun mumbling, breviary held in thick, trembling fingers. Nails chewed down to the pink quick, Rudy noted. Stressful, no doubt, being a priest. He remembered what the paranoically protestant Professor of Tonsorial Artistics had always said about priests: alcoholics or homos, or both; trying to rile his, Rudy's, mother, no doubt, who had been pretty lapsed herself but who had always had a healthy respect for all things clerical.

Father Lacey went on, unintelligibly. Latin, of course. Well, that was all right. He wasn't interested anyway. Rudy waited until he had finished and pronounced, with a sweeping sign of the cross, the benediction which in spite of himself, he fervently hoped would settle on his fevered brow, like a white dove, maybe, and stay there . . .

The main business was over but Rudy didn't want him to go. He didn't want to be left alone. 'What's the weather like?' he asked, to keep him there.

Already half-way to the door, Father Lacey stopped to glance briefly out of the window. 'Some cloud about,' he said. 'It looks like it might . . .'

'I've seen it like that. Dark clouds, and the sea a midnight blue . . . Tell me, are the chokka boats strung out on the horizon like fairy-lights?'

'It's bright daylight out there!' Father Lacey exclaimed. 'It's noon!'

'Why is it so dark in here then?' Rudy asked, suddenly afraid. 'Why is it getting so dark . . .?'

Father Lacey came back to the bed to look closely at him. Wondering whether he should broach the subject of confession again, Rudy suspected; or even – did he want them though? – the last rites.

'It's a sign,' Rudy said fearfully. 'I remember reading about an old schoolmaster, his last words: "It grows dark, boys, you may go home . . ." '

'Yes, well,' Father Lacey tried to comfort him, 'you know you can call on me. I'll tell Sister, although of course they know. They all know. Day or night . . .'

It was comfortable and warm and not unlike being in a regular hospital; he could doze off, he could dream.

Sometimes he was alone, at other times it seemed that Neville and Lyle were there, but everything had become confused and he wasn't sure whether they were really there or just figments of his delirium, his fever dreams. For one thing, they sounded strange, their voices muffled and unearthly, as if they were talking in a vast place, their words echoing from vaulted roof beams to rafters. But perhaps the sound was only in his head, because his head felt huge, his ear canals enormous so that everything, his thoughts, and their voices, boomed and bounced around as if they were all floating under the high buttressed ceiling of a cathedral.

'Said the odour of formalin had permeated his being, preserving his relationships. Said he had to wear a screwed-down skull . . .'

Gladstone! But what was his old bunk-mate doing there? 'Gladstone! You old bum!' he exclaimed.

'Who? What?' Neville, his stick thumping the floor, the sound hollow, like the trump of doom, or some sort of death-knell.

'Wandering, poor soul.' Lyle, softly, sympathetically.

'Gladstone?' Rudy called out. 'I can't see you.'

'It's McNaughton, man! Come to see how you're shaping up.'

Rudy felt himself smiling, his lips stretching, stretching . . . He had to consciously pull them back, will them into shape so that he could speak. 'Oh aye,' he breathed. His mouth was bone dry but his lungs bubbled with mucus. Spit going straight down my gullet, he thought.

'Drowning in his own body fluids.'

Who was that? Not Gladstone. Neville? The doctor?

They were all there, Rudy realised. Come to visit him. He appreciated that.

'Brought Gorman with me, and Herr Reeper.' Gladstone again.

'Herr Grim Reeper,' Rudy murmured.

'Getting morbid.' That was Lyle.

'Bad sign.' Neville, tap-tapping.

'Herr Reeper's come to take you to Berlin.'

'Berlin!'

'Berlin? Great War or the Second?' Some small nostalgic taps on the floor. Muted. Fading.

They were both fading, Neville and Lyle, and he was in Berlin. He had never been in Berlin. But there he was, with Gladstone, because that was where they had promised to meet the old biddy, friend of Herr Reeper . . . She was standing beside a buttress of the cathedral, scattering things, shells and beads and buttons and things. For the gargoyles, he supposed, because there was nothing else around. She looked like a gargoyle herself with the black things, wings, she had sprouting out of her back. Or an angel maybe. Angel of death.

'What's that you've got sprouting out of your back, eh?' he asked her, fly as Fagin. Because he'd recognised her by then. Small sharp birdbody. Queen of the Starlings. Only her voice was all wrong. It wasn't Dean's-widow cultivated. It was old boot. Mavadne, come to haunt him. Birdbody to torment him.

'Me 'blades. When a body gets old flesh and blood shrivel and shrink but the 'blades don't. What's that you've got sprouting out of your shirt?'

'Notebooks. Black as your 'blades.'

'Been writing, have you? Got something down at last, have you? What then?'

'My considered commentary and conclusions. The distillation of a lifetime of observation and experience. Ergo, how to achieve a compromise between socio-politico-religious precepts and the practical requirements of everyday living.'

'Full of old precepts are they?'

'Something like that.'

'Precepts for living? Gawd Gerrie, when you're DYING?'

'Hindsight, you know, when you see it all clearly, at last.'

The boot's voice became sly, salacious, birdbody's eyes sharp, spiteful.

'*What you need, Gerrie Fitzbarry me boyo, is a well-thighed colleen. Breasts like lapwings, flexing and fluttering . . .*'

'Aye. I do 'n' all,' he agreed humbly. 'Flexing and fluttering in my lapwings . . .' Funny, he thought, how much can hinge on a little bit of banter like that. Or become unhinged.

'*Shure now, there's me daughter. Fair hair down to her floating rib, spiky lashes, wild as an unwanted whippet. Never needs to wait for the mood to filter in. Name of little lolloping Lalage. Pretty much out of the ordinary and more than a bargain for any man.*'

'MAVADNE!' he screamed. 'YOU OLD HARPY!'

'Olraait. Hokaaay . . .' Poor Laetitia, genuinely concerned, plumping up his pillows, smoothing down his covers. 'It's only me Kernel, Laetitia, olraaait?'

'Ah, Lalage,' Rudy sighed. 'Skittish one minute. Fey the next . . . like something dreamt up by Peynet . . .'

'What's he on about?' Neville again, spluttering, thumping.

'Said it would be "nice". "Nice" was a word she knew how to use. Never heard it sound so menacing . . .'

'Must be one of his stories,' Lyle said mildly. 'He was a writer, you know.'

'Shaggy as a Shetland pony in winter. Said her mater told her to give me a ride.'

'He's wandering, poor chap.' Lyle again.

'She had 'blades too. Must run in the family. Gave me a ride all right.'

'You old DOG!' Neville, guffawing.

Rudy tried to moisten his lips but his tongue was dry and rough as sandpaper. 'Ah,' he said, 'for the coolness of cantaloupe, or honeydew . . .'

'Cantaloupe? He wants cantaloupe.'

'This time of the year? You're delirious, the pair of you.'

'. . . or the larger silence . . .' Rudy heard nothing more, but he knew it wasn't the larger silence. Not yet.

He saw himself, small, solemn, open-mouthed, front teeth protruding, leaning forward on his chair, his mother beside him, her little black velvet hat pulled down low over one eye and held in place with a large tortoise-shell hatpin, the spotted veil ending just above the beauty spot she had pencilled on her cheek. She was nodding in time with the music, enjoying the old songs favoured by the Male Voice Choir: *Shenandoah*, *All Through the Night*, *Go Down Moses* and *D'ye ken John Peel*.

It was pleasant, sitting there beside his mother, watching the Professor of Tonsorial Artistics warbling away, knowing he'd be in high good humour after the performance, that there would be an icecream in it for him while they had tea.

Strangely though, either the Professor of Tonsorial Artistics' dress shirt was shrinking or he had put on weight because the collar seemed to be far too tight, his face was growing redder and redder, his eyes bulging and not only bulging, but bulging right out at him, Rudy, sitting in the front row.

Just as suddenly the little boy began to grow old. His mother was no longer beside him and the theatre had become a cathedral, the cathedral of his recurring dream, with its high vaulted, echoing ceiling. He was the only person in the audience, shrunken, eyes rheumy, gums masticating, head nodding, wispy white hair plastered down with water. And even as he aged, so did the Male Voice Choir, becoming as wispy haired and rheumy-eyed as he was, keening directly at him: *'Memememememe . . . Aheeeeeeeee . . .'*

'Doan warry, olraaaait?' Laetitia, come to visit him and smooth his sheets although it wasn't part of her duties. 'Your piepie bag is full, darlin', they must bring you a new one, Kernel, hokaaay?'

'Aheeeeeee,' he moaned, joining the mournful chorus, 'Memememememe . . .'

Laetitia, portly as Pavarotti, wearing a voluminous kente cloth gown and waving her brown-flecked handkerchief, transferred to the sanctuary where, moist eyes soulful, she began to sing in a pure contralto, vibrant and rich as Marian Anderson's, with the Male Voice Choir doo-wapping and -wahing behind her:

Then worms'll come an' ate thee oop,

On Ilkley Moor baht 'at . . . she sang, verse after unfaltering verse, in a broad Yorkshire dialect punctuated with Xhosa clicks.

Then shall we all have eaten thee . . .

He began to thrash around spastically, throwing himself forward, staring wide-eyed at Sister Mary Benedict who was attempting to take his pulse.

'No, no, Colonel Knoesen,' she said, squinting with concern. 'That won't do at all. You must try to keep calm now. Shall I call Father Lacey?'

He shook his head, surprised at how weak he had become in so short a time.

'How long have I been lying here?' he asked. 'How long have I been ill?'

'A few days. But if you're wanting to see Father Lacey, he's just up the corridor.'

'Where's the little nurse, the one with the big ears. Thelma.'

'She doesn't work in this section. But the physiotherapist will come in presently to give you a spirit rub and massage your legs and back. We're not needing clots and bedsores now, are we?'

'I'm not up to callisthenics, Sister,' he moaned before dozing off again, his mouth dry and his eyelashes scratchy against his eyeballs.

'*This isn't the way.*' Annie's voice. He recognised it at once.

THE way. Not A way. Clearly what she'd meant to say only he hadn't wanted to listen, that day on the Hill with Claude and the others. He'd been too embarrassed.

Dully he remembered: '*I am the way.*' Could he find it? And hopefully, the truth and the life as well? Turn back from the abyss? Back from the seducing spirits, the very gates of hell? Back to Annie who'd show him the way?

'Annie!' he exclaimed, tears running down his cheeks, down his neck and into the top of his pyjamas, and through them he could see her, Titian-red hair, long white column of a neck, eyes blue-grey as the wintry sea. But she was floating away from him, Annie all in white against a dark sky twinkling with chokka boats, just like a Chagall.

'Annie . . .' he groaned, clutching feebly, trying to get hold of her.

'What is it, Kolonel?'

'I just wanted to say, I never did find it, Annie. There's a barrier, the past come back to haunt me. No more than psychological, probably, but I can't break through. It's the abyss for me. The deep. I just can't make it, a simple leap of faith like that. Too much for me. Can't take a step, not even a small one, not even a child's step . . .'

'What is it then? Kolonel? You're upsetting yourself . . .'

Annie had gone. Annamarie the physiotherapist, with her lank hair and mud-brown eyes, was at his bedside.

'Annie?' he wept.

'It's "Ahna", but you can call me Annie . . . I don't mind.'

'No, no,' he said. 'You don't understand. It was Annie. Herself. I swear . . . Come to show me the way. It's one or the other, you know. It's Annie or the old harpy, the angel of death, with her 'blades.'

The physiotherapist busied herself massaging and manipulating and finally rubbing his back with methylated spirits. The smell reminded him of Zolah. 'Please,' he begged. 'Keep them away from me . . .'

'We're only here to help you. Come on now, Kolonel!'

He was dimly aware of several of the Sisters Mary bustling in and out, of Father Lacey mumbling over him and of Ahna, tirelessly trying to make him as comfortable as possible, and all the while he grew weaker and weaker, his breathing shallower and more laboured.

Everything had become too much for him; he could barely acknowledge the presence of visitors, although he made an effort, especially for old Neville, and Lyle.

'Drawing in, the evenings . . . Although I fancy I can still hear them. The nightjars. And the bats will start squeaking soon . . .'

'Bats all right, if you think those are nightjars!'

He tried to respond, to tell them that he appreciated their visit, that he could feel the evening was drawing in, that it would be dark soon, but the words remained locked in his head for a long time before he was able to manage a hiccup and a whisper: 'It grows dark, boys . . .'

He could feel Lyle bending over him, staring at him. He heard the chair squeak and Neville's stick begin its tap, tapping on the floor; like the raven, Rudy thought, nevermore . . .

He was having to fight for every last shuddering breath now, clawing at the counterpane as he struggled.

He could see the lip of the abyss clearly. Only it wasn't an abyss in the sense of a fissure in the earth, or a canyon – the image he, and probably Annie, had always had in mind. More of a tunnel really, or a sort of funnel ready to catch them all, the tormented, weeping and wailing and gnashing their teeth right down to the depths at the centre, the darkling heart of the darkness, the gates of the shadow of death . . .

He flailed around, struggling to breathe, overwhelmed with anxiety, panicked to the point of hysteria.

'Looking bad, poor old sod.'

'I say.' Lyle, his tone panicky. 'Shall I call somebody? The Sister?'

Call them, he wanted to scream, the Sisters, the Brothers, the Fathers, everybody, call them, can't you see I'm going right down into it, into the very pit . . .

Mucus began to bubble up in his lungs, choking him; terror constricted his throat. Finding the strength from somewhere – in the great reservoir of his fear, perhaps – Rudy fought, face contorted, mouth dry, lips working interminably, tongue darting around in his mouth like a small animal in a hole, demented with thirst, licking at everything. And all the while there was that mucus bubbling at the back of his throat, never rising higher than the epiglottis.

He knew what was keeping him alive: fear of death. He wasn't ready. He hadn't prepared; and the knowledge compelled him to reach for breath after rasping breath, painfully, in a jolting paroxysm of agony.

From time to time he was aware of people in the room with him. He recognised some of them, from the sound of their voices, the things they were saying.

Neville, gruff-voiced: 'He's bought it, poor old soldier.'

He heard Edna Something-or-Other: '. . . when I was sifting through those old newspapers where the mice were breeding, that big black headline, *KENNEDY DEAD* . . .'

'Notable, that was.'

They had come to say goodbye, Rudy realised; or out of curiosity. Not that it mattered.

'I'm jiggered,' he heard himself say.

'He's what?'

'Jiggered. Slang from the Great War. He was a Colonel, you

know. In the Secret Service.'

'Did he say anything about the Salvation Army?' Hot breath on his face. 'You could do worse . . .'

Sister Mary Ambrose leaned over to drape a rosary across his folded hands. 'Comes from Ireland,' she said, 'blessed by His Holiness himself.'

Mumbling and cool drops of water. Ah, Father Lacey, the last rites, the final sprinkling. Sprinkled when he came into the world, sprinkled as he was going out. Too late now to pass on to him the Professor of Tonsorial Artistics' remedy for barber's rash, not that he'd been able to remember it . . .

Silence, except for his breathing, growing shallower and shallower until it was just fluttering, stopping, fluttering heart-stoppingly, until it stopped fluttering for the last, long time.

The next gasping breath had failed to come, and all was still except for his slowly slackening jaw which left his overbite grotesquely exaggerated in death, and the veins of his hands which were swelling out dark blue as the blood trickled down to dam up there.

'Hypostasis,' Sister Mary Benedict explained.

But Rudy couldn't hear her. Ready or not, the larger silence had settled in on him, and just like Kennedy, although not nearly as notably, the Colonel was dead.

Ancestral Voices   Etienne van Heerden

In the wild night hours, or during the heat of the day, when the sun seems to want to drag blood from the very stones, and man's thoughts whirl feverishly – then truth and fantasy, the past and the future, life and death are indiscriminately mingled on Toorberg, home of the Moolman family.

'It reminds one of *One Hundred Years of Solitude* by Garcia Marquez: the history of a country and a nation told in the form of a family chronicle – realistic but visionary, fantastic, mythical.' – J A Dautzenberg, *De Volkskrant*, The Netherlands

'His exploration of personal relations and private lives under the pressure of historical and political forces makes him an eloquent witness of profound social change.' – André Brink

READ MORE IN PENGUIN

Leap Year   Etienne van Heerden

'God would never have designed such a species.' So says Seamus Butler of his famous fall-goats, the result of the genetic strain which his father had inadvertently bred on this Settler family's farm. For these goats have an inborn fault which makes them worth their weight in gold: when startled, they keel over instantly in a dead faint. Thus a single fall-goat placed among a flock of sheep becomes the only prey when an enemy strikes, leaving the flock unharmed.

But it is these pathetic goats, with their mocking yellow eyes, which have given the Butlers wealth and influence in the Eastern Cape – an important factor in a time of great political upheaval, especially when oil is unexpectedly discovered right in the middle of the harbour town of Port Cecil. The discovery and its implications for the town bring into sharp focus the local black civic organisation's demand for a unified city council.

'. . . impressive. As one cannot talk about Israel without having read Amos Oz, or India without Salman Rushdie, or South America without Marquez or Llosa, so you will have to read Van Heerden if you wish to know anything about South Africa . . . . It is fiction at its best.'
– Herman de Coninck, *NRC Handelsblad*, Netherlands

Iron Love   Marguerite Poland

The year is 1913, the place, a boys' school in colonial South Africa. For every boy, the heart of the school is his own House, his Housemaster and his particular Hero. And, for every newboy coming through the hallowed doors, there are two commandments. The first: Silence and Denial. The second: Not to fail at Footer. Validation lies in honouring these. At whatever cost.